I0672014

Dreamin' in '89

A Novel

Praise for *Dreamin' in '89*

"T.G. MONAHAN convincingly conveys the awkwardness and uncertainty of adolescence while he vividly conjures the spirit of the late 1980s in this story of boyhood. The protagonist is especially well portrayed, although readers may question his single-mindedness. Monahan sensitively humanizes bullies, avoiding reducing them to caricatures. A redemption story for a boy whose carelessness has serious consequences, this work takes a fresh and candid approach to classic themes of growing up."

—*The BookLife Prize*

"A captivating storyline with a tumbling twist through a prominent era of history, *Dreamin' in '89* is woven with intriguing scene and characters that make us remember our own youth. The nostalgia, the yearning for more, the longing to be somebody and the realization of what actually matters: friends sticking together and dreams coming to life."

—Chloe Rachel Gallaway
    Author of *The Soulful Child: Twelve Years in the Wilderness*

"*Dreamin' in '89* is outstanding with a well-presented storyline. Amazing author! Amazing book!"

—Javier Ferrea, Retired Aviator, Current Sim Instructor and
    Author of *To Live and Fly in the USA* and *The Gift of Travel*

"*Dreamin' in '89* is a moving tale of one young man's journey to discovering what really matters in life. Faced with constant obstacles and the feeling of being out of control, Seb must learn to face his fears and stand up for himself. T.G. Monahan writes characters who either feel like your best friends or make you want to save them. A joy to read."

—Lorraine K. Toth
    Award-winning Filmmaker, Author, Photographer
    and Pin-up Model

Dreamin' in '89

A Novel

T.G. MONAHAN

This book is a work of fiction. Although it is based on historical events, names, characters, and incidents are either the products of the author's imagination or are used fictitiously. Any resemblance to actual persons, living or dead, or actual events is purely coincidental.

Copyright © 2018 by T.G. Monahan. All rights reserved. Printed in the United States of America. No part of this book may be used or reproduced in any manner whatsoever without written permission except in the case of brief quotations included in critical articles and reviews. For information, address Permissions@CitrinePublishing.com.

Cover design: Rolf Busch · *Author photo:* Lorraine K. Toth

Library of Congress Cataloging-in-Publication Data

Monahan, T.G.
Dreamin' in '89: A Novel

p. cm.
Paperback ISBN: 978-1-947708-12-9
Ebook ISBN: 978-1-947708-13-6
Library of Congress Control Number: 2018952789

10 9 8 7 6 5 4 3 2 1
First Edition, September 2018

 CITRINE PUBLISHING
Asheville, North Carolina, U.S.A.
(828) 585-7030
Publisher@CitrinePublishing.com
www.CitrinePublishing.com

Also by T.G. Monahan

The Vexing Heirloom

i.

SEB, IN THE BACK SEAT, pressed to his sister, wished he was anywhere other than there. In the red sunset, from where he was sitting, his father's hand looked especially gruesome, mangled and splotched with rubbery scars. If only the bandage had not been removed… If only Seb hadn't been so impatient four months ago…

The car sped through the outskirts of Stony Glen town, past the fields where the bigger boys played and the braver boys flirted with girls. They were making terrible time, though. A pile of homework waited at home—homework he'd never get credit for. At least it was just Aloysius and Rob. Timmy still hadn't caught wind.

Kit, Seb's sister, prattled, "You promised."

"I promised we'd look," their mother said, driving. "Three hundred dollars for a dog?"

"Not just any dog," Kit said. "Lucy's special."

Seb said, "Do its new owners know you gave it that name?"

"Stop it."

"That other girl looked *so* happy," Seb said. He glanced at his father. By now, he'd expected a warning glare. But his father just stared out the window.

"We'll have luck somewhere else," his mother said. "Puppies aren't going anywhere."

"But summer is," Kit said. "If it takes too long—"

"We'll do our best." She peeked worriedly at her husband's hand. She'd tried to hide it, but Seb saw.

Kit said, "What if we can't find one?"

Seb enjoyed watching Kit squirm. At eleven, she was just one year his junior, but her desperation made her seem positively infantile. "Newts are on sale at the pet shop," he said. "Or it's another few nights in Ocean City."

His mother's voice sharpened. "There's a hole in my bedroom ceiling..." She looked at Seb's father. "I'm sorry."

His father shifted uncomfortably. His scars, now, didn't look quite so bad: still ugly, but less scary.

Seb chomped his thumbnail. The last time he hadn't delivered on homework, Rob had stolen his lunch for a week and Aloysius had pantsed him in gym class. They'd both smeared glue all over his books. It hadn't always been like this. Nothing had made much sense since...well, it didn't matter since when. Misery loved company. He sneered at pouting Kit and sang, "How much is that doggie in the window..."

She sniveled, "I told you—"

"The one with the waggly tail..."

"Mom!"

His mother said, "Sebastian Riggs!"

"Diane, stop the car," his father said.

Seb gasped. He'd gone too far.

His mother pulled to the side of the road. His father flung the door open. Kit said, "Let him have it." But his father just walked away from the car, into an open field.

Seb followed. His mother and sister's squabbling faded. A high-pitched whining sound rose up. His father pointed skywards. "Look."

Above the field, like dragonflies, two R/C model airplanes droned. One was stubby, red and white, the other longer, red and black. They zipped, then banked, in arcing turns, switching back and forth the lead. Their choreography was flawless, like nimble ballet dancers. A grin, ear to ear, spread across his dad's face, a grin that Seb had only seen when his father was looking at airplanes in flight.

"They're reenacting a famous race," his father said, "the Thompson Trophy in 1932. Jimmy Weddell's Model 44. Jimmy Doolittle in the Gee Bee. The golden age of aviation." He waved to the men across the field, radios slung around their necks, then wiggled his thumbs as if toggling his own. "What I wouldn't give to be your age again, your age and at the stick." His scars seemed almost invisible.

A warm breeze tussled Seb's hair. The airplanes continued their intricate dance. The world, for a moment, seemed magical again, as it hadn't in quite some time. Summer vacation was on its way, Kit would get her stupid dog, Aloysius and Rob's homework was only one night, and he and his dad were cut from one cloth. "Do you think you could teach me how to fly?"

His dad just laughed, "You don't have what it takes."

And just like that his father's scars were back to looking gruesome.

ii.

THE ROAD WENDED UP Woodmansee Hill. The homes were tall, of cultured stone, with kidney pools and wrought-iron fences, and campers parked in car-ports. Usually, Seb liked driving past them, imagining what luxuries lay inside their vine-draped walls. Tonight, they brought no comfort, though. *You don't have what it takes.* It smarted. What did it take? Why didn't he have it?

The trees soared higher. The road switched back, then dipped into the stony glen from which the town had taken its name. Here, the pools were made of tin and sat above-ground, in chain-link fence yards. Boys played stickball in the street, savoring the evening. But Seb chafed like he'd never before. What made his dad and those pilots so special?

They turned onto Dunbar Drive, his street. Stars already flecked the east. Down the block, the fading sun gleamed off his cellar's Bilco doors. "Half an hour," his mother said.

"Fine." He knew what to do. Aloysius and Rob and their homework could wait. He'd show his old man what he was made of. He still had a few minutes of dusk left, too.

The car pulled into the driveway. Chuck was waiting. "Theb," he said.

Seb sprang from the car. "Expect someone else?"

"Um...no—"

"Come with me."

Chuck dropped his bike and followed.

They snaked around the side of the house. A rickety fence separated Seb's backyard from that of the man who lived next door, old Lawrence Vincenti, better known as Ashy Larry for his love of cigars. His neighbor's shed door swung open and shut. Inside was shiny landscaping equipment. "Larry forget to lock up again?" Chuck said.

Seb threw open the Bilco doors, leading down to his own cellar. "He's old and clueless," Seb said. They climbed down the storm-stairs.

The cellar air was mildewy. After four months avoiding it, his dad's workshop seemed strange, as if he was seeing it for the first time. A layer of dust tinged all the machines. A pile of wood and PVC piping lay against the opposite wall, beside two lawnmower engines. Seb felt a pang. One of the boards bore a bloody handprint. He switched on the light. "Help me find it."

"What?"

"An old footlocker." He opened the storage-pantry.

"So you'll never guess," Chuck said. "You know the old diner, next to the airstrip? The one shaped like a blimp."

"Zeppelin," Seb said. He unstacked a pile of trunks. "You're an R/C pilot, aren't you, Chuck?"

"Um...yeah, but..."

"Good," Seb said. "Keep looking."

Chuck gave a perfunctory glance around. "So my grandfather says when they closed down the diner, they donated everything to the library. Souvenirs, pictures, you name it. I hardly ever go there, you see. Once, I checked out this book on gems. I never returned it. I still get bills."

Seb slithered into the crawlspace. The footlocker had to be near.

"Anyway," Chuck went on, "this time, like King Arthur,

I summoned my courage—oh, that reminds me about homework but I'll ask you later..."

Seb's attention drifted in and out. It was always the same with Chuck's shaggy dog stories.

"So I went to the library to see for myself, and sure enough, there it was," Chuck said. "A black and white photo, and it was *him*. He looked old and tired, leaning on a shovel. The ground around him was all dug up. And in writing on the back of the frame...Seb, are you listening?"

Seb's hand brushed against a worn-wood box. "You said flying R/C's easy, right, Chuck?"

"Well, yeah," Chuck said, "I mean, once you get past takeoff."

Seb groped for an edge. "And landing?"

"It's no picnic, but—"

"Then you can do those, just this once—"

"Theb! I was saying I know where it is. Some place called Gypsy Pond."

Seb stopped. "Lloyd Llewellyn's time capsule?" This actually *was* big news.

They'd been searching for the better part of a year. Llewellyn was Stony Glen's number one hero, a flying ace in the First World War. His story loomed larger than life. Legend had it that somewhere in town, he'd buried a time capsule filled with his treasures, including the elusive talisman that gave him his skill and bravery as a pilot. "Ever heard of Gypsy Pond?" Chuck said.

Seb glanced at the window. Day was fading, night falling fast. There was enough time to start exploring. But his father's words still rankled. And Gypsy Pond, wherever it was, wasn't going anywhere. "Remind me how long you've been flying R/C?" He dragged the footlocker from the crawlspace.

Chuck said, "What's gotten into you, Seb? Why does it matter?"

"Because of this." Seb lifted the top. The earthy smell of antique balsa wafted from the box. He pushed aside towels and Styrofoam wedges. Inside was a vintage R/C stunt airplane, lovingly preserved, like relics. Its wings were beige with red racing stripes, its four-channel radio so elaborate it looked as if it might have been the space shuttle's onboard computer. Blazon on the fuselage was the airplane's name:

DREAMIN'

It was once his father's pride and joy. "You can show me, can't you?"

Chuck straightened up. "Um...Oh, yeah. I'm an old pro at these birds."

Seb looked askance. "Birds?"

"It's how we fliers talk. I'll have this ship airborne in five."

Seb looked closer. The servo-horns were naked. "Not without servos connected, you won't."

"Oh, right," Chuck said, "the servers."

"Serv*os*," Seb said. "You know, the motors that let you control it?" Chuck nodded vigorously, almost as if he was trying too hard. "Are you sure?"

"Nothing to it."

Good enough. A sanguine thrill washed over Seb. Chuck would get the plane off the ground, then Seb would take the radio. He'd loop above the boys' stickball game, buzz Ashy Larry's bedroom window. His father was about to learn just what kind of son he had.

He cleared space on his father's workbench. Tools were scattered haphazardly, the same places they'd fallen that fateful day four months ago. His gaze drifted towards the pipes and wood, with its bloody handprint. But that was the past, the Dreamin' the future, the sky the limit for him. He could finally stop looking back.

He strained to lean three iron clamps against the wall above the bench. He shouldn't have been moving them without his father watching. But he was burning daylight. Tonight, all bets were off.

"Why do you need me?" Chuck said. "Looks like you know what you're doing."

Seb lifted the fuselage onto the bench. "Building models, yes," he said. He joined the wings and elevator. "Flying them, no. My dad never showed me."

"And probably won't now because of his ha—"

Seb shot him a glare. "That wasn't my fault." He slid the servos into place, then reached for a screwdriver. "Maybe I'll bring it in tomorrow," he said, "fly at recess, land down the hallway. I can't wait to see the look on old Cornball's face."

Chuck said, "You're actually coming?"

"Why wouldn't I?" Seb tightened a screw.

"I thought you'd heard."

"Heard what?"

Chuck's voice was fraught. "Oh, never mind."

"Spit it out," Seb said. Bad news never got better with age.

"Well," Chuck spluttered, "T.J. told me that Dom told him that Timmy's on to you."

Timmy! Seb's hair stood on end. It was the sum of all sixth-grade fears. His heart raced; he whipped around. "Timmy's *what—?*"

His elbow slammed against the bench. The dusty tools jumped. The big clamps lurched. One by one they crashed to the bench, pulverizing the Dreamin'. Seb stared in disbelief.

"What was that?" Seb's father, upstairs, yelled. He stormed into the cellar. "Haven't I told you not to—"

He froze. His eyes settled on the ruined aircraft.

"Mr. Riggs," Chuck said, "I did it."

Seb's father stood in silence. Faint enough Seb barely saw, he wiggled his thumbs as if at his radio's stick, same as in the roadside field. Then he cupped his mangled hand inside his other hand.

Chuck said, "Mr. Riggs?"

"Go home, Charles," Seb's father said. He hunched above the shattered plane, staring at but past it.

Seb said, "I can fix it."

"Like you fixed *that*." He pointed towards the blood-stained board.

The words bit deep. Seb fought back tears. "That wasn't my—"

"Nothing ever is your fault, is it? Charles, go home. Seb... I don't care." He ran his scarred hand along the wreckage of his prized possession, then trudged up the stairs back into the house.

"I'm sorry," Chuck said. "I tried." He stepped towards the storm stairs.

"Wait," Seb said. Between the bloody wooden board standing ignominiously, and this latest catastrophe, he'd almost forgotten his mortal danger. "Timmy's what?"

"Timmy knows," Chuck said, "about the homework. He wants to know why he got left out."

Timmy was six feet tall and shaved. He'd started school late and been left back, so though he was in seventh grade, he looked like a high school senior. No one dared look in his eyes, and even teachers kept their space. He had a daily quota of beatings. Nerds, like Seb and Chuck, were his favorite.

Chuck said, "See you tomorrow?" He scurried out the Bilco doors.

In the distance wailed a city train, pulling into borough hall. Across the street, the Gallaghers' hound bayed half-heartedly in answer. The coltish taunts of the stickball players, buoyed by thoughts of summer approaching, faded as they dispersed to their homes. All was silence once again, save for the whirr of katydids, as the dusk gave way to night.

Seb looked at the battered Dreamin'. Though crumpled and crushed like an old soda can, it maybe wasn't a total loss. The fuselage-keel remained intact, as did the tail and some of the wings. The engine and servos seemed undamaged. With quality balsa, poplar, and glue, he could probably fix it. Yes—definitely. He'd get Chuck to help him: it was, after all, Chuck's fault it was broken. Right? If Chuck hadn't distracted him during such a delicate task...

Seb clenched his teeth. He'd show his father what stuff he had. He'd show everyone. Right after he finished Aloysius' and Rob's homework.

He closed and locked the Bilco doors, then ran up the stairs into the house. His mother was fastening the blue ceiling-tarp, covering the massive hole that gaped above his parents' bedroom. His father was gathering pillows and sheets and arranging them on the living room couch. Normally, he'd hug them goodnight. But tonight, the less contact, the better. He slunk past unobtrusively and crept inside his bedroom.

Kit was already asleep in her bed, clutching her stuffed animals. He hated sharing a bedroom with her. He'd been thrilled when his father had surprised them all with plans for the upstairs addition. *Now*, he'd thought, he'd have some peace to read his Golden Guides. But then, his father's injury happened and nothing was the same.

He emptied his money jar into his palm, counting off nine one-dollar bills and seventy-six cents in coins. Tomorrow he'd go to Uncle Enza's, the town five-and-dime and modeling store. He had enough to make a decent start: one poplar board to rebuild the bulkheads, three square dowels for the fuselage and wing-flaps, some balsa sticks for assorted repairs, and one tube of wood cement. He'd been saving his money for Ocean City, but this was more important. By week's end the Dreamin' would be good as new.

He pulled off his clothes, slipped into his flannels, and dove beneath his Star Wars sheets. He grabbed his penlight, and Rob's notebook, and set to work at long-division. The math was easy enough for him: he could solve the problems in his head. He stroked the pencil confidently. Last year, kids like Rob had stood in awe of Seb's quick wit. Now, they blew spitballs at him in class and locked him in janitor's closets at recess. And Timmy? What could he possibly want with Seb? What ghastly torture lay in store?

He flipped open Aloysius' notebook. In its margins were doodles of half-naked women and *Guns 'n Roses* lyrics. They didn't make much sense to him. He wasn't cool enough to understand, he guessed. But the Dreamin' would make everything right.

Wouldn't it?

The penlight tumbled from Seb's hand. His eyes were heavy, his grip too weak. His face sank into Aloysius' notebook. It smelled like cigarettes and Tang. For a fleeting moment he saw himself, an R/C pilot, proud and sure, looping over the sun-swept fields, his father smiling admiringly. Tonight had been one huge step backwards. But tomorrow—if he survived—he'd forge two steps ahead.

iii.

T HE GAUZY SILHOUETTE of his mother appeared. "Seb, get up. You're late," she said, and threw his sheets aside. The balmy breath of the late-June morning washed across his legs. Sunlight streamed through slits in his blinds. Bit by bit, last night came back: R/C airplanes, his father's slight, the Dreamin' crushed, and Timmy—

Timmy! He rolled onto his stomach. "Ugh, I feel like death warmed over."

"My luck," she said, "the pilot light's out and we need boiled eggs."

"No," he groaned, "I really—"

"Spare me." She flung him his pants. "In two shakes, Seb."

There was no point resisting: he couldn't duck four days of school, even if it was the last week. He stuffed Aloysius' and Rob's homework into his book-bag, dumped his money jar into his pocket, and pulled his favorite shirt and shoes on. If Timmy was going to murder him, at least he'd look good in the crime scene photos.

He stepped into the living room. The ceiling-tarp billowed above, like a sail. The sky behind it pulsed sapphire-blue. A better day for R/C flying could scarcely have been imagined. Provided he still had use of his limbs, after school he'd go to Uncle Enza's and buy the wood and cement that he needed.

Before the week's end, he'd conquer the sky, at the stick of the refurbished *Dreamin'*. No one would ever doubt him again.

Seb's father was pacing, phone tight to his ear. "I already told you," Seb's father said, "that's too much money down." He looked at Seb, then turned away, and continued speaking into the phone, "None of your business, *why*. It's just that— No. *No...*"

Seb tiptoed into the kitchen. His mother was boiling eggs on the stove. Kit had already eaten her breakfast. Normally, she'd be raring to leave, but she sounded today like an unhinged detective, tearing into a murder suspect. She said to their mother, "You said we'd go before the weekend."

"Some cheese with that whine?" Seb said. Kit blew him a juicy raspberry. Seb stuffed Taylor ham and a croissant in his mouth.

"I'm working a late shift," their mother said.

Kit said, "Then tomorrow."

"Tomorrow night your father has rehab."

"Then—"

"When there's time, Kathryn."

Seb lent his ear towards the living room. He could still hear his dad on the telephone. "Look, I wish I could rush this," his father said. "They just took the bandage off, two days ago. I should be able to start back to work—What? Not until November, at least, and even that's—What does it matter, November or now? All right, please think it over." He slammed the telephone with his good hand, cradling his injured hand in his shirt. This morning, it looked bad again: twisted, pink and red.

Seb feigned a worried stare at Kit. "Haven't you heard?"

"Heard what?"

He said, "It's on the news." His mother glowered from the stove. "Hookworm quarantine," Seb said. "No new dogs in Stony Glen, at least not for a year."

Kit looked despondent. Seb cracked a smile. Kit moaned, "Mom."

"Be quiet," their father said, "you both. Go to school."

"Dad," Seb said, "about last night..."

"Too late," his father answered.

"For what?"

"For school, unless you leave," his mother said. She hurried Seb and Kit out the door.

"Mom," Seb said. "After school, can you drive me—?"

"No," she said. "You're twelve years old." She closed the door behind him. Whether her words were faith or scorn, he could count on little help from her.

Chuck came running, wearing black sunglasses with bright yellow Batman logos. "You're alive," Chuck said. "And actually going?"

Seb pulled the glasses off Chuck's face. "You *want* to get beat up?"

Chuck replaced the glasses. "This Friday can't come fast enough. So I found out more about Llewellyn."

Chuck was a dog with a bone. "Tell me on the way," Seb said. School was just three blocks away, normally a leisurely stroll. This morning, however, they'd have to walk briskly, already five minutes behind schedule. The faster he began the day, the faster it would end, with him fixing the Dreamin'.

"So I asked my grandfather about Gypsy Pond," Chuck said, straggling. "He said it was some old arboretum. People used to swim and fish there."

"Where is it?"

"I'm getting to that," Chuck said, struggling to keep Seb's pace. "It was popular for a long time, but then, he said, something terrible happened."

Seb slowed. "What?"

"One winter night, fifty years ago, two boys snuck inside and fell through the ice. One of them actually froze to death. The other lived but was never the same. After that, the town put it off-limits. They closed it down and fenced it off. Part of the land they turned into a power plant or something. But my grandfather said they never drained it. Gypsy Pond is still out there, somewhere." Chuck flourished his arm, dramatically.

Seb thought about the Stony Glen winters, bitter in their iciness, and what it must feel like to freeze. Llewellyn's time capsule was lighthearted lore, or so he'd always believed. He'd have never expected the tale was tied up with tragedy, even death. "Who was the boy?"

"My grandfather didn't know," Chuck said. "The whole thing was very hush-hush, he said. The boy's family was rich and bribed the newspapers. I guess you can hide from anyone if you're really determined enough."

The façade of Seb's school loomed ominously, like a grim mausoleum, away down the street. Somewhere, inside it, Timmy was lurking. The school day was about to begin— except it wasn't a school day at all, but a gauntlet. And the only way out, Seb knew, was through. "Let's hope," he said, and stepped towards the door.

*   *   *   *   *

Seb, for the fourth time, glanced at the clock, ticking at a glacier's pace, keeping time to old Mr. Cornwall's droning, "One day, King Arthur heard that a friend, King Leodegrance, was going to be attacked by an enemy, the Duke of North Umber. The Duke wanted to take Leodegrance's lands and his beautiful daughter, the princess Guinevere, to be his wife..."

To hell with Leodegrance. The clock said 2:25 p.m. Five measly minutes was all that stood between Seb and the end of the day.

He'd spent all morning planning it. The second the

dismissal-bell rang, he'd slip from the classroom into the hall, then slither out the rear exit. While the others filed to the front, he'd duck into the clump of trees that lined the soccer field, then make a dash to Uncle Enza's. With any luck, he'd be in and out of town before the haughty high schoolers descended, trolling for pizza and kids to torment. It would be the exclamation point on a day avoiding Timmy—

Timmy! If not for that name, the Dreamin' would still be in one piece, he'd be a pilot, and his dad in awe. But he had an opportunity now, not only to fly the Dreamin' but fix it. That much more prestige awaited him.

Chuck, sitting next to him, passed Seb a note. *Stop staring at her,* it read. Seb looked towards the clock. He'd barely noticed: Lauren was sitting beneath it today.

For a moment, Seb's mind drifted into the past: only four months, but it might as well have been Dark Age Britannia, so long ago it seemed. The fastest soccer player in town, hardly a day since Day One of sixth grade had passed without him daydreaming of her. Buoyed by the spirit of Valentine's Day, he'd worked up the nerve to tell her about his special project, the one he was building with his dad. She'd been fascinated, or feigned it well. She'd asked the obligatory follow-ups, and smiled warmly as she did. He'd never forget the way she blushed and played with her hair as they talked about it. When the project was finished, he'd promised himself, he was going to invite her over to see it. But then everything changed, even Lauren, and so much as glancing at her was taboo. He whispered to Chuck, "I'm not staring."

Chuck grabbed the paper, scribbled a new line, and flicked it back to Seb. *You are,* it read. *It's creepy.*

Two months ago, it might've been true. But that was the past; now, Seb needed to focus. He wrote, *Come buy balsa with me after school,* and passed the note to Chuck.

Chuck scribbled more and threw it back. *NASA couldn't fix that thing. And Lauren hates your guts.*

They were the last two things Seb wanted to hear. He crumpled the paper into his pocket and said, "If you hadn't told me about Timmy—"

"Sebastian," Mr. Cornwall said, "would you care to read?"

Every eye in the room turned upon him. Standing, Seb stammered, "Read...What?"

"What are we missing out on there? Care to enlighten us?"

A wisp of laughter rose from the class, delighting in his shame. Seb scanned his text with fretful eyes, sweat beading at his temples. With cracking voice he read aloud, "Um... 'Arthur had met Guinevere once before, and was so struck by her beauty that he felt foolish around her and couldn't speak. He longed to see her again but in such a way that she wouldn't notice him. So Merlin made him a magical cap. When he wore it, Arthur looked like an ordinary gardener's boy. And in this way, he saw Guinevere every day without feeling bashful.

" 'But one morning, when she looked out the window, Guinevere saw a golden knight bathing in her fountain. It was Arthur, who had taken off his cap to wash. When she hurried out to meet him, she found only the gardener's boy, alone, for Arthur had put his cap back on. Guinevere asked where the handsome young knight had gone.

" 'Lady,' Arthur said, 'there has been no one here but me.' "

Seb looked up. The laughter died down. He'd read well enough there was little to mock.

"What does this say about King Arthur?" Mr. Cornwall asked.

Seb threw the clock a furtive glance. Only 2:28 p.m. Time was dragging its feet. "Say?"

"Is he wise? Is he fair?" his teacher said. "How does he treat others, and himself?"

Seb could feel the others' eyes upon him, burning holes in his confidence. Anyone else and they wouldn't have cared, but it was him, and they loved when he failed. Then his glance met Lauren's. Her quick brown eyes and playful smile seemed to belie a secret faith long since snuffed away, he'd thought, or she was a brilliant fake. The last time she'd looked at him that way was....For a moment, it was almost as if the last four months hadn't happened. He'd embarrassed himself enough for one day. "Until he's beaten the Duke of North Umber, he won't be worthy of Guinevere's hand."

A barrage of chuckles and bad imitations of Seb's voice filled the classroom.

"Hmm," Mr. Cornwall said. "Thoughtful, but not what I take from it."

"I'm wrong?" Seb said. His stomach writhed. He'd be taunted about this for days.

"Well, not *wrong*," Mr. Cornwall said, "but not altogether correct, either. Arthur was always destined for greatness, but he hadn't been brought up that way. He's more comfortable in peasant's-rags. He wants his lady to love him on those terms."

Seb looked at the clock, then back at Lauren. She was still grinning at him, her quick eyes buoying his flagging spirits. He took courage. "That's not how he feels at all," Seb said. "What does he have to show for himself? Shiny armor and a sword? He got those from someone else. Until he bests the duke himself, he's got nothing to offer fair Lauren—*ugh!* I mean fair Guinevere—"

The class burst into unrestrained laughter. Lauren's cheeks flushed crimson-red. Old Cornball quipped, "I guess we know where your head was."

R-R-R-R-Ring! The dismissal-bell chimed its shrill aria. Seb had never been so glad to hear it.

"Your homework's to finish King Arthur," Mr. Cornwall said, over a chorus of groans. "You're still mine for three more days."

Lauren grabbed her backpack and rushed towards the door. "Fair Lauren," the others taunted, "fair Lauren."

Seb pushed through the crowd and ran after her. "Lauren, wait," he called.

He stepped into the hallway, already beginning to throng with sixth graders. The seventh graders would be next. His escape-window was rapidly closing. The rear doors behind him stood wide and inviting. He'd be in and out of town with supplies before the high school day let out. But Lauren's face was forlorn. "Lauren," he called again. "Stop. Wait." She scampered off. He turned and gave chase. "Wait—"

Two pairs of arms yanked him backwards, then into the wall. Rob and Aloysius, with cuffed Cavariccis and heavy metal T-shirts, glowered at him, nostrils flared. "Your homework got us detention," Rob said.

Seb said, "But I checked it."

"You were supposed to show your work, numb nuts," Aloysius said. "The old bat knew those weren't our answers."

"Cheating's an art," Rob said. "The ancient art of *illusion.*"

Aloysius aimed a fist at Seb's groin. "What's the capital of Thailand?"

"Bangkok," Seb said, deflecting the blow. "Guys, look, next September—"

"That's a whole six months away," Rob said. "And that's even if we pass summer school."

"Can you imagine that?" Aloysius said. "They want us to come here all summer? How do they expect us to learn anything?"

Seb said, "Maybe if you'd actually done *your* homework—"

"Shut it, dipshit," Rob said. "You had one job."

Aloysius reached inside his backpack, removing a bag of lunchroom chili. "Grade D but edible," he said. "At least, that's what it said on the box."

He'd be picking onions from his hair for days. Seb squirmed to free himself, but Rob pinned him against the wall. "We could let you off the hook," Rob said, "but then we wouldn't be helping you grow—"

"Shit," Aloysius said, and dropped the chili bag. He and Rob grabbed their backpacks and ran.

"Glad they saved the best for me," someone said. Seb turned around.

It was Timmy.

iv.

T IMMY GUFFAWED, "Well, well, well..." He loomed over Seb like a vengeful Goliath.

Seb averted his eyes. To look upon Timmy was death, or a noogie. "I didn't know... I mean, I'm only in sixth, I'm sorry..."

Timmy jammed a wet-willy into Seb's ear. It felt like a slimy, sick little fish. "Well, I'm sorry, too," Timmy said. He grabbed Seb's collar. "Come with me."

Chuck called, "Seb, don't go."

"No choice," Seb said.

"Don't sweat it, schmuck," Timmy said. "You can collect your girlfriend's body later."

He hurried Seb along. Resistance was useless: Seb had blown his chance to escape when he'd followed Lauren. If he hadn't been so scatterbrained, he'd have been halfway to town by now. But Timmy could kill him anywhere. Why was he being spirited off?

Timmy shoved through the dismissal-line, ignoring the crossing-guards' whistles to stop. A white Mercedes pulled to the curb, a platinum blonde in yoga pants and gold hoop-earrings at the wheel. Seb had heard that Timmy's mom was a former fitness model. But he'd had no idea.

"A new friend?" she asked in a saccharine voice.

Seb hesitated. "Yes—"

"No," Timmy snapped, shoving Seb in the car. "Giddyap, now, if you will."

They motored from the parking lot, then through the town, past Uncle Enza's. Seb's spirits flagged even lower. He had no idea where he was going, or what was going to happen. Enza's closed at 5:30 p.m. sharp, and it would be swarming with high schoolers by then. They'd give him a wedgie or dump rocks down his shirt. But he'd take his chances with them before whatever Timmy had in store.

"Learn anything nice at school?" Timmy's mom asked.

"Yeah," Timmy said. "Ever hear of the Spanish Inquisition? They had this thing called the head crusher. If you stepped out of line, or they didn't like you, you got your brain screwed out your mouth."

"Icky," she said. Seb shivered.

The car ascended Woodmansee Hill, tracing the same routes Seb's family had driven less than twenty-four hours ago. Seb scrunched hard against the car door, keeping what distance he could. Last evening seemed a halcyon, long-lost world, where the Dreamin' still worked and Timmy was merely a schoolyard bully, not a kidnapping dungeon-master.

The car turned under a cultured-stone archway, adorned with golden coat-of-arms and several silver letter "V's," then onto a winding driveway, at the end of which stood Timmy's house. A wide, commanding third-floor window revealed a plastic Christmas tree, still standing six months late. Timmy's mother slowed the car, as if to savor the experience. "You boys have fun, fun, fun," she said, oblivious to Seb's impending murder.

Timmy hummed the Beach Boys' tune in Seb's ear as he led him through the garage door.

The house inside was unkempt, smelling like a boys' locker room. Timmy disappeared through a door, then down a flight of stairs. "This way, faggot," he said. Seb followed.

Like a rabbit-warren of hallways and alcoves, Timmy's basement sprawled around him. Timmy motioned him into a rec room. Scattered about were potato chips and dog-eared *Penthouse* magazines. In the corner lay a boneyard of toys: Grimlock the dinosaur Transformer, Castle Grayskull, an old Omnibot, and bins full of Muscle Things and Garbage Pail Kids trading cards. On a desk stood a Commodore 64 computer, and beside it a widescreen television. Timmy switched on a Nintendo console. The din of *Top Gun* shook the house. He pushed Seb into an old recliner, then handed him a packet of papers. "No mistakes," he barked.

Seb unfolded the papers, revealing a set of take-home exams. Each was addressed to "Timothy Vaughn" and each bore a seventh-grade teacher's seal.

"Sweet deal, huh?" Timmy said. "My old man called the school. Fed them some learning-disability crap. They let me have all my finals take-home. Fuckin' A." He reached for his NES Advantage controller.

Seb could hardly believe his eyes. Homework was one thing, but this was high treason. "You want me to take these for you?"

"No, homo," Timmy said, "I want you to tutor me. What the fuck do you think?" He lobbed Seb a pencil. "Get busy."

Seb looked at the topmost exam: seventh grade U.S. History. *Question Number 1,* it read. *Multiple choice. After four bloody years, the Civil War came to an end when the Confederacy surrendered at A) Spotsylvania; B) Gettysburg; C) Appomattox; D) Fredericksburg; or E) Antietam.*

Seb was only in sixth grade, but he'd thumbed through next year's textbook. He hardly ever forgot what he read. He promptly circled *C) Appomattox.*

Timmy said, "Good nerd."

Question Number 2. Fill in the blank. Arrange the following names in the proper order in which President Abraham Lincoln appointed them to command the Union Army. Hint: one name is used twice. A) Pope; B) Meade; C) McClellan; D) Grant; E) Hooker; F) Burnside.

This was easy enough. He started writing *C, A, C, F*—

This was an irredeemable sin. It was bad enough he'd answered one question. One more and there'd be no turning back. He lowered the pencil. "I can't."

Timmy said, "Whatever. You're lucky you still have all your teeth, not telling me about your homework service."

"If I got caught…"

"Afraid you won't get into Yale?"

Seb said, "It's not just that. It's just…well…"

"What?" Timmy said, "That 'permanent record' they threaten us with? That's all a bunch of bullshit. Anyway, my old man'll take care of whatever happens." He pulled a math test from the pile. "This one's due first. Any wrong answers, I'll take them out of your candy ass."

Seb felt his entire body go tense. The longer he stayed here, tests in hand, the more he was complicit. Timmy flailed the controller about, downing imaginary Soviet MIGs in blazes of eight-bit yellow. "Goddam commies!"

There could be no more stalling.

Seb lunged towards the hall. Timmy grabbed Seb's belt and flung him back. "*Bad* nerd," he said. Seb lurched again. Timmy held him down, hand cupped hard against Seb's mouth. Seb struggled and thrashed as a flash of white paper fell from his pants-pocket onto the floor.

Timmy picked it up. "What's this?"

It was the note he'd passed in class with Chuck. Seb reached for it. "Nothing."

Timmy sat on top of Seb, crushing him against the chair. "Well, let's have a look at *nothing.*" His pubescent body odor swirled. " 'Stop staring at her,' " he read, " 'it's creepy. Come buy balsa with me after school?' What the hell is this?" He went on, " 'NASA couldn't fix that thing. And Lauren hates your guts'—Lauren?" His face curled into a demonic leer.

"Lauren DiBella?" He grabbed a cordless phone from its base. "I wonder if she knows about this."

Timmy's fingers pounded the telephone buttons. Whether he was bluffing or really knew Lauren's number, Seb wanted no part of whatever happened next.

He leapt from the rec room into the hallway, then spun the direction he thought the stairs were. Tripping on a Mongoose scooter, he lurched headfirst through another doorway and crashed against a stack of boxes, spilling them, and himself, to the floor. The door slammed shut behind him, plunging him into inky darkness. From somewhere in the basement's bowels, he could hear Timmy's voice. "Oh, yes, Mrs. D, I'd love to..."

Ugh! Could this day get any worse? He fumbled against the wall until his hand brushed against a switch.

Light filled the room; Seb's jaw trundled wide. He was inside a workshop, walls covered with pegboard, surrounded by benches littered with tools: soldering irons, air compressors, and vertical bandsaws, heaped with sawdust. And miracle of miracles, clamped to the rafters or hung from the ceiling, the room was wall-to-wall model airplanes: R/C, control-line, free-flight, and scale. It might as well have been the National Air and Space Museum in miniature.

"There you are," Timmy said. "You're lucky Lauren wasn't home. That means you get another chance." He handed him the tests.

Seb took them, bewildered, still looking around. Timmy said, "What, are you stupid? Never seen a model plane?"

"Not like these," Seb said.

"My father buys them for my brothers and me. Mostly, we just crash them."

Seb looked each airplane over. Almost all were partly broken: cracked propellers, shattered wings, crumpled fuselages. Each was worth more than he could dream of earning inside a year. Who'd have treated them so carelessly?

And then he saw it.

In rapt repose, it hung from the rafters. Its tawny skin gleamed in the fluorescent light, its red racing-stripes like comet's-tails seared in a fiery firmament. Seb's heart thumped, as if he'd seen a ghost. It was even more glorious than the one he'd wrecked.

It was another Dreamin'.

Timmy said, "You like that one? It's a classic from—"

"I know what it is."

Timmy harrumphed, "Well, excuse me, faggot. Didn't realize you were Howard Hughes."

Seb thought about his dad's ruined Dreamin'. True, a pro modeler could probably fix it, but he most assuredly was not that. He'd been lying to himself all day: he'd never finished a build-by-numbers, let alone a vintage stunt plane. The balsa was twice as old as him, the engine and radio obsolete. To try to fix it would be a fool's errand. In a span of less than twenty-four hours, he'd been humiliated by his father twice, destroyed an heirloom, embarrassed Lauren, been roughed up by Aloysius and Rob, and been shanghaied by Timmy. What was left to lose? He could afford to take a chance or two. "Give me *that*," Seb said, pointing at the Dreamin', "and I won't tell Principal Sweeny you asked me to cheat."

Timmy belly-laughed. "Take my tests and I'll let you live." He grabbed Seb's collar and balled his other hand in a fist.

Seb pulled away. "That's my price or I tell Mr. Sweeny."

A hint of fear broke Timmy's rage, then just as quickly vanished. "You go to Sweeny, I tell him about your little side line with Rob and Aloysius."

"They make me do it," Seb said. "There's nothing there for me."

"You sure they'll toe that line? Maybe I'll have a chat with them. We're already in this together, *Seb*, just like Reagan and Gorbachev. Mutually-assured destruction."

Timmy's threat rang true: Aloysius and Rob would lie through their teeth if it meant placating Timmy. And Seb's handwriting *was* on the test. But no one had ever questioned Seb's honesty, and Timmy, Rob, and Aloysius had a lot more to lose than he did. And he needed that beautiful airplane. "I'll take my chances with Sweeny," he said. "Either way..." He let the pages fall to the floor. "I'm not doing *these*."

"Wait," Timmy said, "hold on. I just can't give the plane to you. My brothers would beat me senseless."

Seb said, "Beat *you?*"

"Shut up! I can't give it, but I can *sell* it to you."

That was as good as *no*. "How much?" Seb asked, as if it mattered.

"Three hundred bucks. My brothers couldn't complain about that."

Seb had never seen three hundred dollars, let alone earned it. "Where in the world would I get three hundred friggin' dollars?"

Timmy stepped closer. "Hit a nerve, did I? That's right. You live down in the glen, don't you? Mom drives a Gremlin. Dad's out of work. I heard there's a hole in your living room ceiling—"

"That's enough," Seb said.

Timmy smiled patronizingly. "Tell you what. You keep your mouth shut, I'll let you work for me."

"Work for you?"

"Lawns and yardwork around town. It's good money in the summer. When you finally earn three hundred bucks...." He nodded towards the Dreamin'.

Seb's mind churned. It would take all summer to earn the money, all summer working for *Timmy*. And that was if Timmy kept his word, and his brothers didn't veto the deal. Pro modeler or well-meaning rube, he had a better chance getting airborne fixing his father's broken Dreamin', rather than trying to work off Timmy's. "Not interested," he said.

"Sucks for you," Timmy said. "And just remember your plight. You go to Sweeny, we both go down. You work for me..." He waved his hand like an airplane in flight.

Seb took one last glance at the Dreamin', then hurried up the stairs. The grating strains of *Sally Jessy Raphael* echoed from the living room. Timmy's mom, in purple tights, was exercising to the television. Seb slipped out the garage, then took off down the onyx-smooth driveway, slowing only to catch his reflection in an ornate "V." And as he watched his glum face pass, he wondered if he'd made the right choice.

*   *   *   *   *

The Bilco doors creaked closed behind. Seb stomped down the storm-stairs, bag in hand. He'd made Enza's by the skin of his teeth, and purchased all the supplies he'd needed. He'd even had a bit left over, and bought a roll of Sweet Tarts, to boot. The brushes with Lauren and Timmy had stung, but hope again was running high. He'd already long finished *King Arthur.* Tonight, there was nothing but time, and the Dreamin'. Best to start with the chunkiest pieces, to get himself in a modeling groove, before tackling the finer, delicate parts. He'd first trace the bulkhead on the new poplar, then cut it with a steady hand—

The top of his father's workbench was clear. His father, unobtrusively, was standing just inside the pantry, filling the footlocker with Kit's baby clothes. Seb looked around. "Where is it?"

"Servos and radio still worked," Rich, his father, said.

Seb's entire body tensed, dreading the answer he knew he'd receive. "That's good, right?"

"For the guy who bought the scrap." Rich lifted the footlocker into the pantry. "No one ever made an omelet without breaking some eggs."

"Excuse me?"

"Think about it."

Seb said, "But I bought—"

"Your mother needs all the help she can get." Rich fastened the footlocker.

Seb held the bag open. "This was less than ten dollars."

Rich only shook his head. "You're part of the solution or part of the problem. Here's hoping you know which is which." He closed the pantry door, then walked up the stairs into the house.

A sickening sense of déjà vu washed across Seb, head to toe: shamed yet again, and the Dreamin' sold for scrap. His father's warning about their money echoed unusually bleak in his ears. But louder, even, echoed the gauntlet he'd thrown down just one day ago.

You don't have what it takes.

Yes, he did.

Yes. He did.

Now, there was only one thing to do.

Seb laid the bag down, careful not to crack anything, and made sure the receipt was still inside. He slipped up the stairs, into the kitchen, where his mother and father sat at the table, poring over a pile of bills. He rifled through the pencil-drawer for his school's telephone directory. His father didn't know it yet, but his days of agonizing were numbered. Soon, he'd be watching his flying-ace son, bursting with pride with every trick turned.

Seb zeroed in on, then slowly dialed, the telephone number. A saccharine voice answered, "Hello?"

He swallowed in a stone-dry throat. "Is Timmy there?" he asked.

V.

THE CLOCK, a wearied sentry, ticked its last 2:30 p.m., surrendering to summer break in the scream of the dismissal-bell. For a moment, time stood still, the grim travails of sixth grade congealing into memories, only to be shoved aside by June, July, and August. Seb launched from his desk and raced down the hall, amidst the cheers of happy kids, bound for beaches, camps, and pools.

"Seb," Chuck called, "what about Gypsy Pond?"

"Not today," he said. "I caught my first job!"

He burst through the main door onto his Huffy, then shot from the parking lot into the road, and into the great American work force. Every honest moment's toil would inch him closer to the Dreamin'. By summer's end, with any luck, a new flyboy would rule the skies.

The streets of Stony Glen were thronged, order melting into strife, the rhythms of the old school year expiring in freedom. Boys dipped French fries in milkshakes and spun their ball caps backwards. Girls with iridescent socks rolled up rocked headphones in the crosswalks. Teachers and crossing-guards, shorn of their mantles, wandered aimlessly, like ghosts. And in the air, above it all, the strains of Poison and Paula Abdul rang out like treacly theme music. But it all blurred gray in the sides of Seb's eyes. He was bound for bigger things.

Outside of town, the bustle subsided. Seb turned off the main drag into Fox Hollow, one of the new developments. Here the homes were opulent, with soft cream siding and dogwood trees, and monogrammed flags with Gothic script. Unlike the homes atop the hill, they all seemed very much the same. He counted mailboxes until he'd reached number one hundred and twenty-six. Timmy was waiting, arms folded. "Hurry up, gaylord," he said. "You're late."

Seb's watch read 2:40 p.m. "I'm five minutes early."

"You're on Timmy Time now, pipsqueak. Early is never early enough."

Seb gazed over the property. The front lawn was lush and perfectly square, last mowed in checkerboard cross-hatches. Past white picket gates on each side, the backyard sprawled to a hemlock hedgerow, encircling the lot. Timmy led him to his gear-laden golf cart: riding lawnmower still hitched to the cart, string-trimmer, electric hedge clipper, and gasoline jug. Seb leaned on the mower's wheel.

"Dream on," Timmy said. He plugged the hedge clipper into a cord. "Know how to use this?"

Seb looked over the hemlocks again. The hedge seemed endless, tall and thick. But someday, his Dreamin' would soar even higher. "I'll figure it out."

Timmy demonstrated. "Parallel to the hedge, perpendicular to the ground. Your math dork ass ought to understand that." He held the power cord up to Seb's face. "Cut this and I cut your dick, assuming I could find it."

Seb took the clippers, squeezing the trigger. It whirred in his hands, nearly tumbling from his grasp. Timmy shook his head and sighed, "Another adventure begins."

The teeth of the clippers tore through the hemlocks. The carnage piled at Seb's feet. His arms, unused to it, burned as they'd never: not even in Pee Wee League, three years ago, when he'd been a starting pitcher, back when he lived for sports.

The sun began its westward slide, still hot enough, though, Seb wished he'd brought water. Timmy, oblivious, goaded the mower, like a Zamboni driver on ice, banging his head and beating fake drums to the sound of Prince through his headphones. Seb could recognize the song: that annoying Bat-rap from the upcoming movie that had everybody, himself included, on edge. The town theater, even, was decked yellow and black. Last summer's big movie, *Who Framed Roger Rabbit?,* was nothing compared to this new spectacle. But nothing, Seb knew, would ever compare to the spectacle of him at the stick of the Dreamin'.

A flash of color caught Seb's eye. A group of girls was walking towards Timmy. And Lauren was among them.

Seb's heart slammed into his throat. She'd been shunning him since Monday. He stared intently at the hedge, pretending not to notice her. Then Timmy shouted something at him, inaudible over the clipper's growl. Seb released the trigger. "Huh?"

Timmy called, "Come over."

The reckoning was at hand, like Luke confronting Vader. He trudged their way, eyes on the ground. The Dreamin' would make it all right, someday. He had to hold fast to that.

Timmy put his arm around Seb. "Ladies, meet my new protégé. Quick on his feet and works like a beaver."

Seb pored over the words for a moment, trying to locate the insult in what sounded strangely like a compliment. "Um...thank you?"

"You bet."

He glanced at Lauren. He could swear he saw the hint of a smile, which dithered and fluttered mysteriously the longer he watched, just like the Mona Lisa. He stood up straight and wiped his brow. "My turn on the mower, boss."

Timmy chuckled, "Not quite, champ," and handed him the string-trimmer. "Edges tight. Don't waste the string." He pushed him towards the sidewalk.

Seb walked towards the lawn's edge, flush with relief. He laid the string against the grass and squeezed against the trigger. The girls waved at Timmy and went on their way, traipsing towards the outskirts of town. Timmy resumed lawn-mowing, tracing the lines of the cross-hatch pattern, surely as Katarina Witt had traced figures at Calgary. The string-trimmer whined, devouring grass, carving a neatly squared-off edge. For a moment, Seb thought, the world seemed hopeful, like the smell of new-fallen rain when a storm gives way to sun. Inside his smelly preteen hulk, maybe Timmy had a heart. Maybe, just maybe, working for Timmy wouldn't be the ordeal Seb had thought.

He finished trimming and walked towards the mower. "Timmy?"

"How 'bout 'Mr. Vaughn'?"

Nope. Timmy was evil. Might as well embrace the suck. Seb held out the string-trimmer. "Done."

Timmy examined the nylon string, then dug through his pockets, producing a wad of crumpled bills. "There."

Seb took the money. "This is just six."

"Be grateful I paid you at all," Timmy said.

"Three-fifty per hour," Seb said. "That was our deal, remember?"

"Yeah, but you've got to see it from my shoes. I'm running a business here. The wheel of commerce doesn't slow because you think you got short-changed." He pointed at his landscaping tools. "Overhead, and wear and tear. You think hauling all this shit around town in a golf cart is cheap? Someone's gotta buy gasoline. Someone's gotta maintain this stuff."

"It should be you."

"There *is* no me. Only us." He crossed his fingers in mock-solidarity. "Besides, you work too fast. Time's money, shithead. Next time, slow it down a bit. We want to milk these suckers." He shooed Seb away with a flick of his hand.

The awful realizations crashed: Timmy wasn't the dunce he let everyone think, and Seb was in bed with the devil. It wasn't too late to back out. But who else had a Dreamin' to sell?

Seb boarded his Huffy, then stopped. He'd almost forgotten. "Timmy?"

He grunted, "Mr. Vaughn."

Even Seb had his limit. "You didn't tell her, did you, Timmy?"

Timmy said, "You think she doesn't already know?"

Whatever he meant—whatever *it* meant—Seb wasn't rightly sure.

He glided slowly down the street, rustling the bills in his pocket. It should have been ten dollars and he one-thirtieth the way towards the Dreamin'. But Timmy was Timmy, and money was money, and he at least had made a start. He'd begun the day with an empty bank jar. He'd go to sleep with something more.

The ranch-dotted byways fed to Boulder Road, Stony Glen's main artery, thrust arrow-like through the center of town. The hordes that had filled it hours ago had mostly dispersed, no doubt to the fields, where Stony Glen was playing Hawthorn in the opening night of Summer League. Seb drifted leisurely past the store-fronts, each a portal to a world in miniature, the apple of some shopkeeper's eye. But as he rode, a familiar gait caught his glance.

It was his mother. And she was carrying one of her lladros.

He rode closer, unobtrusively. His mom disappeared inside the pawn shop. Careful not to be seen, Seb slunk into the adjacent alley and came to a stop beside the door that led to the pawn shop's office. It was slightly ajar, to let in the breeze. He held his breath and listened.

"I hate to make things worse, Diane," Rand, the pawn-broker, said.

"*You're* not," she said. "It's this or Ocean City."

A pang of fear arced along Seb's neck. He lived for Ocean City summers.

"My girl's desperate for a puppy," she said. "I couldn't buy a hamster. Rich's hand won't be well until spring. He says November. He's kidding himself."

Seb thought about his father's hand, mangled and, for the time being, useless. Rand said, "And your son?"

His mom exhaled. "Still blames himself. Dumb *Boy's Living* scam. The funny thing is..." She hesitated, voice cracking. Seb steeled himself for what she'd say. "The funny thing is," she said, "I'm not sure he *isn't* to blame—"

Seb spun aside, away from the door... and into Aloysius' arms. "Lookie what the dog dragged in," Aloysius said.

Seb broke free and turned to ride. Rob appeared at the alley's mouth, blocking his escape. "Time to pay the drummer," Rob said.

He tried to be cool. "Guys," he said, "long time, no see. And it's cat and piper."

"Shut it," Rob said. "We still have a bone to pick. Was *that* metaphor to your liking?"

Aloysius re-grabbed him. "The old bat told Sweeny we'd been cheating. We were already going to summer school. Now we have to repeat seventh-grade math."

"You're fucking lucky Timmy likes you," Rob said. "He said if we dropped a dime on you we could consider our asses grass."

Seb said, "Good old Timmy."

"Not so fast," Aloysius said. "All he said was we couldn't tell Sweeny. Which means..."

Rob slammed his fist in his hand. "Do I hear open season?"

Seb feinted sideways, then threw one of his dollar bills to the ground. Both Aloysius and Rob lunged for it, snorting half-intelligible grunts about Snickers bars and baseball cards. Seb thrust his foot to his bicycle pedal and sped on down the alley.

"Get back here!" they called. Seb looked behind. Aloysius and Rob were boarding their bikes, a GT Performer and a Mongoose Grand Prix, snickering menacingly.

He pedaled hard down townhouse row, then into the industrial park. Trying to head for home would be useless; Aloysius and Rob knew all the streets, and he didn't want to take the chance his mother might see him being tormented.

"No wonder he's so fast," Rob called. "Fairies fly!"

Beyond the highway, the line of Old Grant Hill loomed large, gateway to the Ramapough Highlands. The trees on the east slope grew tall and thick. He could lose them in the brush.

"Here we come!"

He sped down the main drag, then hooked into a hairpin turn, zipping under the old archway that once welcomed airplane and automobile workers. The old factories sat shattered and sad, their once-lush campus home to weeds, here and there dotted with dead Cessna frames and hulks of Studebakers.

"Closer and closer!"

Seb zigged and zagged through warehouse alleys, scraping his knees on cement walls and skinning his legs on the chain of his bike. Ahead, just past the Beechcraft plant, the road led from the industrial park to the catwalk over the highway. Seb pumped his pedals for dear life, gasping for breath with searing lungs.

"No escape!" Aloysius said.

Seb sped across the catwalk. A clump of old, ramshackle houses gave way to woods, then a muddy ridge, traversed by a winding path. He pedaled frantically up the incline, Aloysius and Rob still fast on his heels. "Game's up, Crasher," they called out. "Leader-1 and Turbo have you surrounded."

He crested the hill. Before him spread the ruined bones

of the old municipal power plant, long since abandoned, reclaimed by the woods. The sun was in full freefall now, dragging evening in its wake. Good thing he'd paid attention in science class. He knew Aloysius and Rob had not.

He jumped off his bike and stashed it. The glint of sunlight off its frame blended with the aluminum fence. Rob and Aloysius crested the hill. Seb crouched low behind a tree, orienting himself due west, directly beneath the sun. He was hardly concealed at all, but the light in Rob's and Aloysius' eyes gave him all the cover he needed. They cupped their hands into visors.

"Where are you, faggot?" Rob called.

"No fair," Aloysius said. "We just want to talk."

Seb held stone-still. He could hear the blood in his temples pounding like hammers.

"We ain't done with you," Rob said. He flung a rock into the trees. It landed only inches away. "Better sleep with one eye open." They swung their bikes and rode downhill.

Seb held his crouch a few moments longer, lest Aloysius and Rob be bluffing. A millipede crawled up his leg. He helped it back into the leaves. The woods here, at the edge of town, were foreboding and drab, unlike his familiar haunts; a remnant of the primeval forest that once covered the continent, where Indians lived and settlers dared. Ten minutes had been all the difference between pinnacle and doldrums: now he was a dollar short, and maybe no Ocean City vacation. And that wasn't even the worst of it. *I'm not sure he* isn't *to blame,* his mother had said. She'd been generous.

Of course he was to blame.

He rose, and stepped back towards his bike. His foot caught something. He fell to the ground.

Seb dusted the mud and burrs from his clothes, then looked at the ground where he'd stumbled. Something odd was hidden there. He cleared away the rotten leaves and pulled it from the loam. A legion of beetles and centipedes scattered. He lifted the thing up to his eyes.

It was an old, corroded metal sign, long reclaimed by the elements. But a whit or two of paint remained, still legible to nimble eyes.

This way to Gypsy Pond, it read.

vi.

CHUCK SPREAD THE MAP on Seb's father's workbench. The legend read *Stony Glen, New Jersey, 1980.* "Show me where," Chuck said. He was burned to a crisp from two weeks down the shore. Normally, Seb would've been jealous, but now he was too preoccupied.

He scanned the roads and land formations, looking for a familiar point. Beginning in the center of town, he traced the path Aloysius and Rob had chased him until it reached the catwalk. The lines of streets abruptly stopped, giving way to ridges and draws, dotted by water features. "Here."

"Which pond?" Chuck said.

"All I saw was a sign."

"Llewellyn was wily. We'll have to pound ground." Chuck grinned eagerly. "Tomorrow?"

Seb looked away. "I can't."

"Ugh," Chuck groaned, "Timmy? I heard his house was built on a Hessian graveyard. His cellar is filled with bodies, they say, all encrusted with topaz and jade."

"I doubt it," Seb said. There was only one thing in Timmy's basement that interested him: the vintage model in the rafters, so close yet still so far away. "Just thirty bucks in two whole weeks of work."

"Man, has it been that long?" Chuck said. "I'm still on Wildwood time. At that rate it'll take two summers."

"Friggin' wear and tear," Seb said. "He docks me every time, says I wear out his equipment."

"Tell your mom."

"Sure, that'll work."

"Tell *his* mom."

"What color is the sky in your world?" Seb said.

"There are plenty of other jobs," Chuck said. "You could work at the snack bar at the pool or caddy at the golf course. You'd earn three hundred a lot faster."

"Yeah, but Timmy wouldn't sell. He wants my money *and* my labor. If I want the Dreamin', I have to play ball."

"Well, you know best," Chuck said. "So, day after tomorrow?"

"Can't either," Seb replied.

"We *are* going sometime, aren't we?" He stepped towards Seb. "Can you promise me at least—*Whoa!*"

He'd stumbled over a dowel. Chuck flailed for something to regain his balance. The back of his hand thumped the table saw's button. With a scream, the old saw roared to life.

Seb froze. All at once it was February 17, 1989, a date seared forever into Seb's brain. He'd stood beside the table saw. His father stood over it, cutting, as he had a thousand times—only this time, it was late at night, his father exhausted from the upstairs construction. Winter had been unseasonably warm. A solid six days without any snow had prompted his father to take the risk he could frame the new rooms inside of a week. But the project had bogged down in unforeseen details. And, dammit, Seb wanted his *Boy's Living* hovercraft finished before spring. Though tired to the point of tears, his father refused to break his word. Then, in a scream and splatter of red, two lives would never be the same.

Chuck hit the "off" button. "Sorry," he said.

Seb came to. "It's all right."

The upstairs cellar door swung wide. Seb's father's voice boomed, "*Again?*" He thundered down the stairs.

"It was an accident," Seb said.

"It's no accident if it keeps happening."

Chuck stepped between them. "Mr. Riggs, ever heard of Gypsy Pond?"

His father scowled and looked at the map. "I'm tired of this bullshit, Seb. Lloyd Llewellyn and model planes? When I was your age I had a job. Your mother has *two*."

"I have a job," Seb said.

"Slaving for that rich kid for pennies to blow on candy and comics isn't a job. It's a waste of time."

"Says you."

His father scoffed. "If I'd said that to my old man..." He cradled his injured hand in his other. "Let's just say justice would've been swift. But that's my fault, not yours, I guess."

Chuck said again, "Mr. Riggs..."

"It's a myth, Charles." He wagged a finger in Seb's face. "You're part of this family, son. You could at least acknowledge the mess you've made. You've obviously no interest in helping clean it." He turned up the stairs. "Stay out of my shop. That goes for you both."

The door slammed. Its boom reverberated, giving way to awkward silence.

"I'd better go," Chuck said. He rolled the map and tucked it away, then climbed to the Bilco doors. "Next week, maybe?"

"We'll see," Seb said. But he already knew he wouldn't have time. Timmy had jobs planned for each day.

"Well, what about *Batman?*" Chuck said. "At least your nights are free, aren't they?"

Even longer than he and Chuck had vowed to find Llewellyn's talisman, they'd yearned for the moment they'd see *Batman* together. As the Joker, Jack Nicholson was an inspired choice, and Kim Basinger was, well...Kim Basinger. But who knew what the next weeks would bring? "We'll make it work," Seb said. He hoped time wouldn't make him a liar.

"Hmm..." Chuck said, and scurried off.

Seb shut the lights, climbed the stairs, and closed the Bilco doors behind. The evening was sultry, humid and bright. The field crickets chirped their whimsical ensemble as brown bats fluttered in the eaves. The Gallagher hound barked at slow passers-by on evening constitutionals. The energy of the living earth was wild and palpable. Somewhere, nearby, maybe even his street, lives were being forever changed. Boys and girls were enjoying first kisses, double plays, triple ice cream scoops. Moviegoers were being enthralled by the Bat and sports fans by the bash-brothers' Oakland *A's*. Seb couldn't shake the nagging uncertainty.

Was he missing out?

No. The Dreamin' was his trophy, his bride. His father had no idea. And someday after he'd grown up, he and his *own* son would fly it, together.

But Chuck was right. At the rate he was getting paid, accounting for his week in Ocean City—if that was even happening now—there was no way he'd have the Dreamin' this summer. The harder he worked, the more Timmy skimmed. He needed an edge, and needed it soon.

"Seba*steen?*" came a rollicking Italian accent.

Seb turned. Ashy Larry was standing in his back doorway. "Mr. Vincenti," Seb said. "Hey."

The old man took a drag of a Cuban cigar, his stash of which was local legend. "It's Larry," he said. "You're old enough."

The honor took Seb by surprise. His neighbor had always seemed so dense. "Thank you?"

"No mention it. So..." He drew another drag. "Any plans for summer?"

Funny he should ask. "Mostly just working. Trying to make enough to buy an airplane."

Larry winced. "A little young, aren't you?"

"A *model* airplane."

"Well, good," Larry said. "When I was your age, I loved airplanes. Eddie O'Hare, the *Enola Gay,* Chuck Yeager and *Glamorous Glennis.* Those were the days. Anyway..." He drew and heaved another puff. "Between a rock and a hard place, Seb, then as far as your feet will carry you. That's where you'll find what really matters."

The words rattled around Seb's brain, bouncing against the odd revelation that Larry, too, was an aficionado of aviation. "Wait," he said. But Larry was gone.

Seb stood alone. The night breeze whispered past his ears, swaying the boughs of his neighbors' tall oaks and rustling the overgrown grass in the vacant home catercorner from his. The hinges of Ashy Larry's shed, trundling open and closed with the wind, groaned from behind the fence across the yard. Larry had forgotten to lock it again.

Seb peered through the fence, inside the shed. Moonlight danced among the teeth of Larry's electric hedge-clipper and gleamed like ice on his gas-powered string-trimmer. The old man's house was dark, and still. He'd never be the wiser.

"Wear and tear, my ass," Seb said. He knew what he'd do.

vii.

SEB PULLED ON HIS PANTS and old denim shirt, less stealthy than he'd have to be if Kit was still asleep in their room, but quiet enough not to wake his parents. He glanced at his sister's empty bed. Where was Kit anyway? Where could an eleven-year-old have gone before 6:00 a.m.? It wasn't like her to vanish so early, and without word to anyone. Each day, his world grew topsy-turvier.

He peeked through his window blinds. The east pulsed a gaudy pink. *Red sky in morning, sailor take warning.* But he was no sailor. And it was Timmy who'd be wise to take warning. If everything went according to plan, Seb's days of pinching for crumbs were over. Timmy would have to deal with him straight.

He crept towards the door. His foot caught one of Kit's stupid stuffed animals, spilling him against his desk. He caught the edge and steadied himself. A magazine tumbled to the floor. Seb held his breath and listened. His parents were still asleep. He bent to lift the magazine.

A shock shot through his body. It was a *Boy's Living*—the *Boy's Living*—the issue that had started it all and led, via dark and twisting path, to him getting ready to steal. Well, not *steal.* Borrow, really. He was sure Ashy Larry wouldn't mind, and anyway, he'd never know. No one had ever made an omelet without breaking some eggs, he'd been told. The Dreamin' was his omelet. It would all be worth it.

He replaced the magazine, stepped through the doorway, and strode fast but lightly across the living room, snoring parents in his wake. He slipped through the kitchen, turned the back doorknob, and secreted himself outside of his house. He gently closed the door behind: he'd passed the first of three obstacles. The upcoming two would be much harder, though.

The backyard was bathed in the flush of twilight. The squabbling of the catbirds and crows would lend a cover of sound to his deed, but only if he hastened. He licked his lips: this was crossing a line; a line not easily crossed back. But the time for dithering had passed. Summer was fast exsanguinating. He stepped lightly across his lawn, then slithered under the rickety fence that separated his yard from Ashy Larry's. Popping up on the other side, he scanned both right and left for danger, then leapt to his feet and inside the shed.

The air was musty, tinged with motor oil and decades-old wood. All around was landscaping equipment: lawnmowers and post-hole diggers and bags of Kentucky blue grass-seed. It was hard to believe even fuddy-duddy Larry would fail to secure such items for long. But the Dreamin' was worth taking the risk.

He opened the shed's back window. Up close, the plan still looked viable. The property behind Larry's, with which it shared a fence, was vacant and on the real estate market. Its backyard was overgrown with wildflowers and crabgrass: the perfect place to hide a string-trimmer, if only for an hour or two. The plan was a go. He unscrewed the cap from a gasoline can—

The lights in Ashy Larry's house popped on.

Seb ducked behind an old milk can. The sun had not quite filled out the sky; the roseate curtain of dawn still hung, undrawn, above the west. Behind the glare on the rear windows, Seb could see the old man's form, shuffling around his kitchen.

Seb's heart raced. He couldn't hide in the shed forever. Timmy would be expecting him, and to blow off Timmy would mean getting fired. But he couldn't just make a mad dash. Stepping out the shed's front door, he might as well be playing the tuba, so obvious it'd be. And though he'd been told he was small for his age, he wasn't squeezing through the window. Just like Mafatu from *Call It Courage,* he was trapped on hostile turf.

He fretted. Anxious moments ticked away. The eastern sky turned turquoise blue; the western sky oozed golden. Ashy Larry shambled about, thick cigar in hand. Daylight, soon, would unfurl its banners. Then his neighbors would be awake and, by and by, his parents. He had but precious moments left.

"Damn," he said. This had been an awful idea. He should have gone in the middle of the night, under cover of darkness. He pressed on the floor to winch himself upwards—

He recoiled, then retched at bit in his throat. Behind him and along the floor, the rancid smell of decaying wood was especially pronounced. An arresting notion crossed his mind. He'd lived through enough rain-flooded basements to know what happened to wood when soaked.

He sniffed along the floorboards, then moved aside an old push-mower. In the meager light through the back window, he could see black splotches in the wall and telltale signs of termites. While the wood everywhere was damp and rotten, here it was positively disintegrated.

He could pry the panel loose.

He peeked back towards the kitchen windows. Ashy Larry still lurked about but was none the wiser.

Seb laid his hands on the panel and pressed. A mouse

skittered across the floor. Seb gritted his teeth and replaced his hands. The pulpy pus of moldy wood squished between his fingers. A house centipede slunk over his foot. He licked his lips and drew deep breath, and heaved the panel from the frame.

Other than a muffled thud, its falling made no sound. Seb poked his head through the gap in the wall. The rear fence was only feet away, and cut high enough he could slide the trimmer beneath it. He banished thoughts of mere escape. The plan was still a go.

He slipped back inside the shed and filled the trimmer with gasoline. He grabbed a pair of bungee cords and secured the front door from inside. Knowing Ashy Larry, if he found the shed locked from inside, he'd probably just ignore it, hoping the problem would fix itself or one of his sons eventually would, by which time Seb would have returned the trimmer. His chest fluttered as he drew shallow breaths. All this for a model airplane? But no! It was infinitely more than that. He slithered out the hole in the wall, then pulled the trimmer after him. He slipped the trimmer under the fence, then replaced the felled paneling. Tomorrow, he'd return by dark. The plan would live another day. The Dreamin' would not have long to wait.

He squeezed back into his own backyard. Careful not to alert his parents, he commando-crawled along the ground and to his kitchen door. He turned the knob and slipped inside. In the mirror, he flashed a smug smile. He'd only one obstacle left.

"Seb," came his mom's voice, "you're awake too. Seems both my brood are early birds. Unlike someone else I know." She playfully poked Seb's father. Rich groaned and rolled back over.

She stepped into the kitchen. She poured two bowls of Double Chex, then filled them both with milk. Seb grabbed a spoon and began eating.

"This is uncharted turf for him," she said, pointing at Seb's father. "He's always been Mr. Fix-it. But if this drags on..." She motioned towards the ceiling tarp. "I'm afraid of what he might end up doing. Anyway, I'm proud of you. I know this can't be easy."

But the hollowness in her voice rang through. And Seb remembered, clear as day, what she'd told the pawnbroker. "Ocean City will seem like heaven," he said.

He waited in vain for a response. She chewed her cereal in silence. "Where's your sister?" she asked at length.

"Try the pound," he said. "Or the pawn shop."

She dumped her cereal bowl in the sink. "Make the most of your teenage years, Seb." She disappeared into the house.

For a gnawing moment, he parsed her words. His mother was nothing if not direct; speaking in riddles was not her style. But little in life still obeyed the old rules. His was a fearsome, volatile world, like the one King Arthur was born into, but destined to make right again and bring about the golden days. That would begin with the Dreamin'.

He stepped outside, mounted his bike, and rode around the block. By now, the neighbors were awake: he'd have to be even stealthier. He rode onto the vacant lot. The warm air hummed with the droning of bees, darting among the crabgrass and thistles, and chattering squirrels chasing each other around the maple trees. He grabbed the string-trimmer and laid it across his handlebars. Then with all deliberate speed, he blew from the backyard and into the street.

The wind whipped triumphantly along his face. He'd survived the gauntlet. He'd passed all pitfalls unscathed, like Indiana Jones and the Holy Grail. Returning the trimmer would be quite something else, but he was sure he'd figure it out. He could figure *anything* out.

He stuck to the side ways, keeping a low profile. Through gaps between houses, he could see to the downtown, where workers were hoisting banners up buildings. He squinted to read:

Stony Glen Summer Jubilee
Friday, August 25 – Sunday, August 27, 1989

Once, he'd loved the Summer Jubilee, with its Tilt-a-Whirl and corn-toss games, its foot-long franks and soft pretzels, its being the only time each year his mother let him eat cotton candy. This year, however, he dreaded it. Everybody would be there: Aloysius and Rob, Timmy's family, and, of course, fair Lauren. That was three good enough reasons to avoid it like death. He'd rather have his molars drilled.

But that was still a month away. By then, no doubt, he'd have the Dreamin'. Then, he'd be a boss.

He wheeled his bike onto Merck Avenue, then down the block to number sixteen. Timmy, waiting, turned as he neared. His jaw, punctuated by the slightest of grins, trundled low against his chest.

Seb dismounted his Huffy. He lifted the string-trimmer over his head, like some Medieval jousting champ.

"About that wheel of commerce," he said.

viii.

JULY IS A WORLD APART, a refuge from the dull routine, a haven from what's commonplace, a month pickpocketed from time. July is fireworks and song, baseball games, blockbuster films, and zany, twisting waterslides in crisp, blue swimming pools. July is the cherry ice, cleansing fast fatigued palates, wearied long of bitter bites of the humdrum hardscrabble. July is the exclamation point affixed to the end of the schoolyear sentence, the stage on which the fondest plans ripen into memories, for summertime obeys no rules and permits everything.

But Seb's days marched lockstep, predictably. Each afternoon was passed in toil, pushing lawnmowers or trimming hedges, or helping Timmy do the same. A great day's haul was fifteen dollars, an average between seven and ten. Timmy and Seb exchanged few words: not for a moment did Seb think they were friends. But a grudging respect had clotted between them. Seb had Timmy to thank for his gains and even though he'd never admit it, Seb knew that Timmy needed him, too.

And that was a good thing, for the home front was not, his house more obstacle course than haven. Most mornings found Kit oddly absent, no doubt off pining for her elusive dog; every third or fourth night saw one less lladro in his mother's collection, newly arranged to mask its shrinking. Evenings brought no family time, not even Friday evenings. His mother, working two hospital shifts, floated about the house like a wraith, subsisting on coffee and Whatchama-callits, too tired to escape from Kit, too stubborn to give in to her. Dinners were joyless affairs that dripped tension, between his sister's bratty whines, his mother's nodding off in her plate, and always his father's judging glare, belittling him without words, whether or not his father meant to. He maintained a wide enough berth from his father, not so much out of terror or guilt, but from a need to demonstrate how far he'd come. Inside his sweat-soaked, Timmy-funded chrysalis, magical things were happening. When the moment was right, he'd step in the light of his father's esteem and bask in its warmth.

Not that that was his only trial. Dodging Chuck had become his other profession, so persistent his friend had become. Chuck had no summer job, unless video games or bumming around the town pool counted. Before he'd started working for Timmy, Seb had never noticed or cared if other kids had jobs. But between cleaning hedge-clipper cuts, pushing lawnmowers up mountainous hills, and getting back to it, exhausted, each morning, Seb had come to see the world through new and less carefree eyes. Gypsy Pond and Llewellyn's time capsule—and even, maybe, Chuck himself—had come to seem like wastes of time, pitfalls along the way to his goal. But he still needed Chuck to teach him to fly. And now he knew just what he'd do.

Boulder Road led clear from one end of town to the other. From the edge of Woodmansee Hill, Chuck would do the initial takeoff, then turn the radio over to Seb. He'd circle about the gilded mansions, turning the heads of rich ladies sunbathing, then ride his bike along Boulder Road, ever his hands at the radio slung round his neck, until by and by, with no fuel left, he'd bring her in for a dramatic landing down Lloyd Llewellyn's old airstrip. The whole town would be there, waiting to see the new Santos-Dumont, the latter-day Lindbergh, thundering his balsa wood Valkyrie to a triumphant stop. His father would throw his arms skyward and cheer that his son was a man, in his footsteps. And maybe, just maybe, Lauren would be there, too, with a kiss from her lips to her bold Rickenbacker.

This vista, so splendid, Seb played in his mind's-eye day after day, carrying him through monotonous toil in the gardens of dentists, bankers, and lawyers as July bled lustily towards August.

*   *   *   *   *

Dusk found Seb and Chuck at the duck pond, swinging old branches like medieval swords. Between them, Seb was always King Arthur; Chuck, ever dutiful, a milquetoast Mordred. The evening resounded with the quacking of mallards, frolicking on the opposite bank. Dodging Chuck meant sometimes giving in, to take the edge of his friend's neediness. A few minutes here, an hour there: enough to briefly slake Chuck's thirst, lest he start stalking Seb at work.

"So he rescues Vicky Vale," Chuck said, thrusting, "and escapes with a grappling hook. Then the Joker—and this is my favorite part—says something like... get this... *How's he get such wonderful toys?*"

Seb parried. "When does he fly the Batwing?"

"I don't want to spoil it," Chuck said. "On guard!" He lunged.

Seb coolly turned the strike. Chuck fell. Seb reached out his hand. "Gentilesse," he said, "for a fallen foe," and pulled Chuck to his feet. He could hear the old swagger return to his voice, like lyrics to a nursery rhyme.

Chuck brushed mud off his knees. "We could see it tonight if you want."

Seb had had his fill of Chuck for one day. "Not tonight. My dad...um...has rehab."

"So?"

"So, my mom needs me to watch Kit." It sounded plausible enough.

"Well, we're still going to see it, together, right? I mean, it's been out for a month. I tried to wait for you."

"Definitely," Seb replied, as he had the last hundred times Chuck asked.

"And Gypsy Pond?"

The other bee in Chuck's bonnet. Seb said, "Maybe tomorrow, after the Osur job. This one's really important. It'll be all day at a single job. I'm at two hundred and seventy-five dollars now. With any luck..."

"Wow," Chuck said, "that quickly? Three weeks ago you said—"

"Things have changed." Ashy Larry's equipment had made all the difference. Cleaning and sneaking them back to the shed nightly was a pain, but it had paid off handsomely. Timmy could no longer stiff him, and now he could take double the number of jobs.

Chuck pointed towards Seb's bike, where Ashy Larry's string-trimmer leaned. "I guess you had it out with Timmy. He lets you take his equipment home."

"Sure," Seb said. Telling Chuck would be as good as telling the whole town. "Well, get ready."

Chuck drew a blank. "For what?"

"For teaching me to fly, of course."

"Oh, yeah," Chuck said, looking down at his feet. "About that—"

"Get down!"

They dropped to the ground. Across the brook, Aloysius and Rob appeared, skulking silently. But those two were always loud and obnoxious. Seb whispered, "What are they doing?"

Aloysius and Rob headed towards the mallards' nests and crouched behind the cattails. Rob pulled out a Zippo lighter, flicking it on and off with his thumb. Aloysius reached for something as well. Seb squinted, to see clearer.

It was an M-80 Salute.

The mallards went about quacking as ever, oblivious to approaching peril. A chill ran up Seb's spine. He remembered Rob bragging about fireworks, snuck into town across state lines. Shaking Seb down for homework was one thing, but this was something else. "We have to do something."

Chuck fretted, "No way. Cornball said don't play with fire. Remember Icarus?"

"He also said always do the right thing."

"But our fingers—"

"*Quiet.*" Seb covered Chuck's mouth. Aloysius and Rob leered down at the ducks, then touched the Salute to the flame.

Chuck said, "I can't watch." He buried his face in his arms.

Seb thought of *Make Room for Ducklings.* It had been one of his childhood favorites, a special occasion when his dad would read it. His dad would sling his big arm around him. Seb would always snuggle near, convinced there was no safer place in the world. Time and the *Boy's Living* hovercraft tragedy had tarnished that assuredness. But anyone badass enough to fly the Dreamin' across Stony Glen, then land on the airstrip to cheers from his dad and a kiss from Lauren, was badass enough to do the right thing, even if just for a bunch of ducklings.

He rocked back and forth on the balls of his feet, then whispered to Chuck, "You're my witness." Aloysius lobbed the Salute.

Seb burst from the cattails, across the embankment. Rob and Aloysius cried, "Faggot! What do you think you're doing?"

Seb splashed into the water. It felt warm and slimy, like the town kiddie pool, filled with sunblock and pee. A few yards away, the ducks milled about, close to the fizzling Salute. Seb churned his legs for all he was worth. He'd have only about five seconds more.

"Scram!" Rob yelled, slinging a rock at his head.

The rock stung, glancing Seb's ear, but he was not about to retreat. He waved his arms and roared, "*Tiltowait*," his favorite spell from *Wizardry*. The ducks burst hither and tither each way, flapping and quacking and scrambling for safety. He flung himself onto the ground.

Boom! The Salute blew with a mighty thud. Seb could feel it in his bones. Behind a plume of blue phosphorescence, a crater in the mud gaped wide. But not one feather had been harmed.

"Fucking ass," Rob said, "spoiling our experiment."

"How are we supposed to learn about percussion now?" Aloysius said. "*Whoa—!*"

The embankment beneath their feet collapsed. Aloysius and Rob tumbled face-first to the mud. "Ask and you'll receive," Seb said.

He turned and raced up the opposite bank to where his bicycle was staged. Chuck was already waiting there, fretting and panicked as usual. Seb grabbed Ashy Larry's string-trimmer, mounted his bike, and pedaled away. Behind him, Chuck's voice shrieked, "Wait up!" Farther behind but gaining speed, he could hear Aloysius and Rob giving chase. But this time, Seb thought, whatever they were fixing to do to him didn't seem quite so daunting.

ix.

SEB LEAPT OUT OF BED at break of day. A bright, new, happier world was dawning. With any luck, by day's end, the Dreamin' would be his.

He tiptoed to the closet. For the third time this week, Kit was already gone; bed made, stuffed toys emplaced. Where could she be going? Probably cruising the shelters for strays or trying to talk breeders out of their runts. Her desperation was almost cute. He shrugged and donned his landscaping duds, then slipped through the living room, into the kitchen, and—

He screeched to a halt. His father was standing at the sink. Seb couldn't tell if he was awake or sleepwalking. "Dad?"

Rich stared into space. "No one ever warns you," he said, "that the two worst things you can possibly have are a dream and all the time in the world to see it go to waste." He cradled his injured hand.

Seb's shock wore off. It wasn't like his dad to speak in riddles. "Huh?"

Rich's stern bearing returned. "Your grandfather fought in Korea," he said. "I wasn't much younger than you. Before he left, we were going to buy a TV. Instead, my brothers and I did odd jobs around town, and gave our mother whatever we earned."

"Generous," Seb said. He knew what Rich was angling at.

"I'm glad you think so," Rich replied, and disappeared into the house.

But life, today, was just too damn good. Victory was imminent. Seb wasn't about to be ambushed with guilt. His father didn't know it yet, but his days looking past his son were numbered. Seb grabbed a banana and a poppy-seed bagel, and slipped unobtrusively out the side door.

The cicadas had begun to stir, warming the cacophony that would ring the skies through mid-September. Summer vacation was nearing its peak, to begin the slow roll to autumn. In the best of worlds, the thought would have rankled but now, Dreamin'-less and on borrowed time, each moment seemed a precious gem, to be strip-mined of its maximum worth. Good thing the wait was almost over.

He checked to see the coast was clear, no neighbors skulking or peeking. He slithered under the rickety fence, then slipped inside Larry's shed. As he'd done every day for three weeks now, he filled the string-trimmer with gasoline, then secreted it out the window. Closing the door behind, he crept to the trimmer, then stuffed it under the white vinyl fence, obscuring it in the overgrown grass. One short bike ride later, he was back at the fence-line, retrieving the trimmer, then off like a shot to his latest job site.

Timmy appeared to grin when he pulled up, though Seb knew it was for the trimmer, not him. "Big day," Timmy said, and lobbed him a water.

Seb plucked it mid-air, still holding the trimmer, and set his bicycle down in the driveway. "*The* big day," Seb said.

"Don't count your chickens yet," Timmy said. "This old coot's a cheapskate."

From where they were standing, a cobblestone driveway wended its way across a brook to an apple orchard, punc-tuated dead-center by a gingerbread-trimmed bungalow. "Looks like it paid off for him," Seb said.

Timmy said, "Nah. The town gave him this house, for all the Krauts he killed. As if that made any difference."

Seb knew Mr. Osur from town parades. A soldier in the second world war, his was a place of honor on the veterans' float. "Sounds pretty brave."

"You would think that, faggot. Brave would be making people money." He gestured towards the hedge. "Speaking of which..."

Timmy, like stone, was unchangeable. But nothing today would squash Seb's spirits: the Dreamin' was only just out of reach. He had only to extend his will, and trim the hedges and weeds.

Morning expired in a golden flourish, giving way to sweltering noon. August was nearly upon him now, and it'd be a month Seb would never forget. He'd put back, for the last time, Larry's string-trimmer and never borrow it again. Who knew? Maybe he'd do the old man a solid, to square themselves up anonymously. But whether or not he ever saw fit, in a matter of days, if not mere hours, he'd be a bona fide R/C pilot. Like the skyward pioneers of old—Alcock and Brown, Lindbergh and Bennett, and Stony Glen's own Lloyd Llewellyn—he'd chart his own course through the pages of lore, winning love and accolades. Then his world could truly rewind to a time when everything made sense.

Evening's raggedy shadows spread. Seb admired his day's handiwork. Timmy was gathering up his equipment. He peeled off several bills. "Good work." Seb counted the money, then drew a deep, delicious breath.

He'd done it.

"Twenty-five," Seb said. "Which means—"

"Which means I'll see your ass at ten. Mrs. Phillips' house."

"Which means I have three hundred." He stared at Timmy a pregnant moment, then waved his hand like an airplane in flight.

"Oh," Timmy grumbled, *"that."*

It was as surprising as it was ominous. Seb said, "You remember?"

"Sorta."

Timmy was too smart to have forgotten, and there'd have been no point playing dumb. "Sort of *what?*"

He looked away. "You've got your cash."

"To give back to you," Seb said, "for the plane." Actually putting it into words drove home what an awful deal it had been. But he'd performed. It was Timmy's turn now. "Well?"

Timmy nibbled a fingernail. "I'll, um...have to ask my brothers."

"You haven't already?"

A hint of fear crossed Timmy's face, same as Seb had seen in his basement, only more pronounced, but quickly replaced by his usual scowl. "Mrs. Phillips' tomorrow at ten." He wedged his headphones onto his ears. "Better get going before your bedtime."

Cold sweat beaded at Seb's temples. Timmy hadn't actually said no but he hadn't said yes, either. The uncertainty would devour him. "Just tell me—"

"Bye." Timmy clicked on Michael Jackson full-volume and threw a clippings-bag over his shoulder.

A panic began to swell in Seb's brow, tingling its way across his scalp, then down the length of his spinal cord. *I'll have to ask my brothers.* The worry branched off in two, down both legs. Shouldn't Timmy have done that already? Could Timmy have swindled him?

"Young man?"

The voice was so faint he almost missed it.

"Young man," it repeated. Seb turned. Mr. Osur was peeking out his back door. "Come closer," the old man said. "I have something for you."

Seb peeked over his shoulder. Timmy, music blaring, was lugging clippings to the curb. Warily, Seb stepped towards

Osur. Even pushing seventy years old, his presence was daunting. "Yes?"

He shook Seb's hand. It was firm and felt like crepe paper. "So sorry."

"Huh?"

"I heard you two arguing. I don't know you, but I know Timmy. I've seen how he treats his workers. Look..." He pointed at Ashy Larry's string-trimmer. "He's making you use your own tools."

"Well, um... actually—"

"Pish." Mr. Osur raised a twenty-dollar bill. "For any troubles."

He hesitated, then peeked back towards Timmy. "Um..."

"Please," the old man said, and pressed the money into Seb's hand. "My dear wife, Lord rest her soul, would never let me live it down."

Seb felt a pang of guilt. To take it seemed slimy: he and Timmy had agreed to disclose and evenly split any tips. But they'd also agreed, at least Seb had thought, that Timmy would sell him the Dreamin'. Now, it seemed, all bets were off. He stuffed the bill into his pocket. "Thanks."

"Come back soon," Mr. Osur said, and slipped inside his house. Seb mounted his bike and pedaled away.

The evening was balmy, filled with glad voices: barbecues and softball games, and children slurping cherry ice. Seb fidgeted with the money he'd made: forty-five dollars to add to his stash, bringing him to three hundred and twenty dollars, but the nagging question just festered the more. Might it all have been for naught? He tried to picture the Dreamin's first flight, turning heads across the town, his father's pride, and Lauren's kiss. But the reverie, a broken reel, only sputtered before his mind's-eye. Would Timmy deliver on their pact? *Could* he deliver on their pact? Would he even try to?

He pedaled harder. The vision of his plane's maiden voyage grew murkier with each block passed. He'd gambled all on Timmy's pledge, or what he took to have been a pledge. He'd given up his summer vacation, or a good chunk of it. He'd brushed aside his only friend and the quest for Llewellyn's time capsule. In the loosest possible meaning of the term, he'd been borrowing his neighbor's equipment. He'd just pocketed twenty dollars in ill-gotten gains. No one had ever made an omelet without breaking some eggs—that much, according to his dad, was true. But his eyes had been firmly fixed on the omelet. He'd never considered what breaking eggs meant until he'd bothered to look at the carnage.

But he damn well shouldn't have had to.

Twenty bucks was no skin off old Osur's back. Larry would never catch on to the scheme. And Timmy? Screw Timmy. Timmy had forced him into this fix, skimming off and abusing Seb from the start. Timmy had roped him into this job, itself just a few shades better than serfdom. Hell, Timmy's own *name,* uttered by Chuck, had ruined his father's original Dreamin'. Timmy had better come through for him. No, Timmy damn well *would* come through for him. And however Seb had to make sure that happened, having the Dreamin' would justify it. Fucking A it would!

Wouldn't it?

"Well, well," came a voice, "if it isn't Launchpad McQuack?"

Aloysius and Rob cut him off in the street.

𝒳.

SEB LURCHED to a grinding stop. He tensed his legs to pedal for life, then thought the better and let them slacken. Aloysius and Rob were all smoke and mirrors. There was nothing they could do to him unless he allowed it. "What?"

Rob said, "You still owe us."

"I owe you jack," Seb said. "Now move."

"Ooh," Aloysius said. "Every rose really *does* have its thorn."

"Bite me," Seb said. "Get out of my way."

Rob said, "Got any more of that cold hard cash?"

Seb waved his forty-five dollars about. "All in a day's work. Not like you'd know."

"Why work when you can scam?" Rob said.

"Ixnay, dumbass," Aloysius said, then turned to Seb with a mawkish frown. "Got any plans for tonight?"

Immediately, Seb regretted showing off his money. "Um..."

"You see *Batman* yet, dude?"

By this point, Seb was maybe the only human alive who hadn't. Even his mother and father had seen it, and Chuck had gone five or six times. He'd made a promise to see it with Chuck, but that was long past moot.

"I hear it's awesome," Aloysius said.

Truth be told, it was getting impossible to avoid spoilers. *Batman* was everywhere: collectors' items, T-shirts, even Bat-signal buzz haircuts. Though still going strong, it wouldn't forever. And then it'd probably be another year until the VHS.

"I wanna bang Kim Basinger," Rob said, hips gyrating, "Woof!"

Aloysius said, "Cool it." He turned to Seb. "Well?"

From where Seb was standing, obscured by Summer Jubilee banners, he could see past the train station to the downtown. A line had formed outside the theater, short enough that they all could likely still get in if they hurried. But Chuck or no Chuck, this wasn't how he'd imagined it. And he'd have to leave his bike and trimmer, with no way to secure either. "Why would I take you two to the movies?"

"Because if you do," Rob said, "you'll be cool."

Two months ago, that might have made hay. But the Seb of two months ago was gone. "Take a hike—"

He bit the word short. A flash of kelly-green soccer jersey, split by a chestnut ponytail, caught his eye. It was Lauren. And she was in line for the movie theater.

"Okay, guys," Seb said. He could feel the words escaping his lips, as if he wasn't so much speaking them as getting out of their way. "Let's go."

Rob grinned. "We were wrong about this dude."

"Indeed," Aloysius said.

They walked to the theater, its art deco façade in the throes of Batmania. Aloysius and Rob took their place in the line. Seb led his bike into the alley. He grabbed an old rope from the ground and tied the trimmer and bike to a dumpster. He covered them both with burlap sacks. It wasn't a safeguard by any means, but it was Stony Glen, after all. How much could go wrong in two hours?

"Hurry up, dude," Aloysius called. "It's almost our turn."

Seb ran to the line. Lauren was already inside the theater. He recognized the ticket seller: Charlotte, the woman who checked badges at the town pool. The town kids made a puerile game of sneaking past her turnstile. "Almost full," she called out.

"Don't sweat it," Rob said. "We'll let you know how we liked it."

Seb stepped to the window and put down his money. "Three for *Batman,* please."

The machine spat out two tickets. Aloysius and Rob snatched them up, then pushed past Seb into the lobby.

"Last two," Charlotte said, handing five dollars back. "Next show's at ten-fifteen."

Seb's heart sank. Ten-fifteen was way too late. From his vantage, he could still see Lauren, milling inside the lobby. A few weeks ago, he'd compared her to Guinevere, but he'd been dead wrong.

The comparison hardly did her justice.

"Just one more, please," he said. "I'll even stand if I have to. Please."

"That's a fire hazard, sweetie. Ten-fifteen."

King Arthur wouldn't have given up. "No." He pushed the money back towards Charlotte. "Please. I'm begging you. It has to be this show." He glanced at Lauren again. She was laughing with her friends.

Charlotte sneered cynically. "You know the three rings of marriage, son? Engagement ring, wedding ring, and suf*fering.*" She pressed a button. The machine spat a ticket. "Good luck finding a seat, Romeo."

Seb grabbed the ticket. "Thank you. No more turnstile-hopping for me."

He raced inside the lobby, thronging with teenagers and kids his own age. Most were wearing *Batman* shirts, yellow Bat-logos against a black field; some had even bleached their faces, red lips and green hair à la the Joker. His eyes scanned the length of the room for Lauren. A flash of green past the theater doors belied her having entered.

"Hey, duck defender," Rob called. "Me and the homeboy here be famished." He motioned Seb towards the concession stand.

"Fine," Seb said. He stepped to the counter, eyes fixed in the theater, trying to figure where Lauren was sitting. The clock on the wall read 7:58 p.m. The theater was rapidly filling with viewers. In the chaos, he could catch only snippets of words, coming from Aloysius and Rob.

"Popcorn with butter, milk duds, nerds, mello-yello..."

He focused on the glitter of green. For a moment, he felt like that millionaire, Gatsby; the one he would read about in high school, or so old Cornball had assured him. He'd stared at a green light across a bay, or something, until that light had lost all its meaning and the love of his life had broken his heart. He dreaded the thought of being in high school. Cool kids like Lauren would be at home there, but he would still be—

"Seb!" He looked up. Rob was staring at him. "Pay the good man."

"Oh, right." Seb reached into his pocket, then looked back in the theater. He could still see the green of Lauren's jersey, meaning the rows around her were clear—for now. He pulled out his money.

"In that case," Rob said, "make them large."

What? "Huh—?"

A roar rose from the crowd. Darkness fell across the room. Aloysius and Rob grabbed their sodas and snacks and tore off into the theater. In the gathering artificial night, Seb squinted to cleave to that lifeline of green.

"Hey," the vendor said, "your change."

Seb stuck his hand out, gaze still fixed on Lauren. He felt his palm fill with bills and change. He wadded them deep inside his pocket, then raced inside as the previews came on.

He darted between moviegoers. "Excuse me," he said, "beg your pardon...comin' through." One or two he may have nudged, or possibly even pushed, but it was all in the service of something greater. He sidled into an empty seat between two older men, but only two rows behind Lauren, with a perfect view of her. Limned by the trailer for *The Abyss*, her hair and profile made her seem every inch an angel.

"Fire at will! Fire at will!"

Aloysius and Rob were lobbing milk duds at unsuspecting kids. Adults were issuing stern warnings. Seb couldn't help but feel responsible: he'd bought those milk duds, after all. He glanced back at Lauren. He'd done it for her. And so they would think he was cool.

The theater went pitch-black. And then Seb learned what "cool" really was.

Danny Elfman's theme music soared. A terrified street thug begged, "What are you?" A black vigilante declared to the world in growling monotone his identity as *Batman*.

Seb was transfixed as never before. Crooked gangsters and pinstriped hitmen. An embattled mayor and district attorney. A zany reporter and his partner, the scintillating Vicky Vale. A mysterious millionaire with a secret. A clown prince of crime and his lethal nerve gas. A showdown for the ages, played out in the gray and twisted byways of that signature hellscape, Gotham City.

Seb strayed out of time and space. Two hours disappeared into the ether.

Then all at once the bright Bat-signal pierced the noxious, gloomy sky, a beacon of hope and strength and goodness amidst a sinful, fallen world. And all at once Seb would never forget, the name of "cool" was *Batman*.

The credits rolled, the lights came on. But Seb could only clutch his armrests and draw shallow, choppy breaths of popcorn-scented air.

"Hey, kid." An usher holding a broom and dustpan was

staring at him from the end of the row. "Some time tonight, maybe? We got next show in fifteen."

Seb looked out over the theater. His fugue subsided; he sank back to earth. The theater was almost empty of viewers. Aloysius and Rob had long slithered off, their pockets full of milk duds and nerds. And Lauren, too, was gone.

He jumped from his seat and raced up the aisle, then burst into the lobby. She couldn't have vanished that quickly, could she? Only the Bat with his smoke grenades could make such stealthy disappearances.

Had she caught a second feature? He peeked into the small theater, interrupting *Ghostbusters II,* but she was not inside. The ladies' room, perhaps? He sidled to the vestibule, fixing his eyes on the restroom doors. But after five minutes, she hadn't emerged. He had missed a golden chance.

Seb hung his head. *Batman* was all he'd hoped it would be, and even so much more. He should have been smoldering with verve. He should have been rehearsing lines, to recite when he next saw Chuck. But all he felt was dejection—

"Seb?"

He turned. It was *her.*

He stumbled backwards. Her soccer ensemble and black-strappy Mary-Janes were the pinnacle of junior-high chic. She smiled and flipped her ponytail back. He stammered, "Guinevere! No, wait...I mean...I mean...." He threw up his hands. "You know how sorry I am about that, right?"

She laughed. "Enjoying your hovercraft?"

It'd been months since he'd told her about that. "You remembered?"

Her brown eyes crinkled. "I want to take a ride—"

"Lauren!" Her friends grabbed and dragged her away.

"Call me when it's finished," she said.

"You'll be first," he said, half-whispered, as she vanished past the door.

There was no hovercraft, nor would there ever be. But in some parallel dimension, where February 17, 1989, had come and gone with barely a second thought, Seb and Lauren were making plans for an afternoon of hovercraft rides. And that was all that ever mattered.

A puffy pink cloud floated up beside him, then all at once morphed into the Batwing—only it wasn't the Batwing but a life-sized Dreamin', painted like Batman's aircraft. In a decorative mirror, Seb caught his reflection. He was clad head to toe in black body armor, cowl and cape with bright yellow emblem, fierce and redoubtable as fuck. "Open," he said. The canopy slid back. Inside was Vicky Vale, dressed in green. But it wasn't Vicky Vale. It was his fair Lauren. "Hold on," he said in his Bruce Wayne-esque snarl. The canopy slid shut. Lauren grabbed his gauntleted hand. The Batwing/Dreamin' blasted off, into the cloudy night.

He throttled along Boulder Road, scattering high school kids as he flew, grinning with his manliest sneer as they dove for cover into the gutters. Lauren laughed along with him. Ahead, running scared, were Aloysius and Rob, smack in the middle of the street. Seb nudged the aircraft flush to the ground and unsheathed its two .50-cal machine guns. Aloysius and Rob wailed, shitting their pants. Seb shot up the road to the tips of their shoes, then chortled as they jumped down a manhole quailing in terror.

He looked at Lauren. She'd approved.

He zoomed past homes to the outskirts of town. The people cheered out; all villains fled. Then off in the distance, something appeared: a peculiar blob of purple and green, going just as fast as him. Lauren went ashen. Seb approached. It was the Joker mounted aboard a lawnmower, only it wasn't the Joker at all. It was Timmy—

The reverie shattered, the dream dissipated. The Batwing turned to a sooty cloud, then vanished into vapors. Seb was in the alley beside the theater.

He reached into his pocket. All that was left was a handful of change and two single dollar bills. In his haste to sit close to Lauren, he'd let Aloysius and Rob blow his money. He was twenty-five dollars short of three hundred. He could no longer afford the Dreamin'.

He looked down. At his feet lay a pile of old burlap sacks and the stump of a rope with its end frayed away.

His bike and Larry's string-trimmer were gone.

xi.

SEB'S FEET, in worn work boots, throbbed on the pavement, sprinting to the morning's job site. The balm of the late-July mist brought no comfort. He'd never adjust to a life with no Huffy. And without Larry's string-trimmer, it was back to Timmy scheming and skimming, and he had to make up twenty-five dollars.

He did some quick computations. At his old rate of three dollars per hour, given the number of jobs they'd booked, it was likely he'd earn it back in a week. Then, assuming Timmy was selling, he'd immediately buy the Dreamin'. He'd keep it a secret for a while, as not to arouse his parents' suspicions. Hopefully, the geezer next door wouldn't notice his trimmer was missing. And if he did, by then, Seb would have thought up a good alibi.

From the fog loomed Timmy's silhouette, standing in Mrs. Phillips' driveway. "You're late," he said. "Where's the trimmer?"

Seb said, "Not today."

"Whatever," Timmy said. "I wasn't paying your ass anyhow."

Seb, hunched and gasping, felt himself go queasy. "Come again?"

"You heard me. I saw Osur tip you."

He hadn't been sly enough yesterday. "I don't know what you're—"

"Don't bullshit me. How much?"

By now he should've known Timmy couldn't be bluffed. "Just twenty bucks."

Timmy said, *"Just* twenty bucks? What's one good reason not to fire you?"

"Well..."

"Don't say you were going to tell me."

Damn. "No," Seb said, changing course, "I was—"

"And don't say you were going to buy gas for the trimmer."

Damn, Timmy really was sharp. Seb could only stammer, "No, I...um—"

"In fact," Timmy said, "just shut your fool mouth. I've made up my mind anyhow. You can go."

Seb's mind set to swirling, a maelstrom of dread. Everything seemed to be coming undone: money, bike, trimmer, and now job—all gone. But he wasn't about to surrender his last, best chance at the Dreamin'. "No."

Timmy turned. "No?"

"You heard me." There was no point holding back. "We had a deal."

"You made your three hundred."

"It was never about money," Seb said. "It was about the plane you'd sell me."

"I never promised you that."

True, Timmy had never *promised* he'd sell, and his brothers could have kiboshed the deal. But the implication had been clear. So Timmy had led him on for six weeks. "Now who's bullshitting who?" Seb said. "I wonder if Mr. Sweeny's around."

"Oh, that's rich," Timmy scoffed, a faint glint of fear in the side of his eye. "I already passed all those tests. You've got nothing on me, faggot."

"We'll see." Seb held out his arms like two balance-scales. "Repeat seventh grade again or make three hundred bucks. Hmm..."

"Jesus Christ," Timmy said. "All you are is a pain in my ass. Meet me at the fields tonight. 6:00 p.m., and don't be late. Bring the three hundred." He spat a wad of Big League Chew.

Seb exhaled. He'd won. In spite of all the odds, he'd won. "6:00 p.m.?"

Timmy stormed off. "Fuck you."

*   *   *   *   *

Seb raced up the orange shag carpet stairs, then burst into Chuck's bedroom. It had been a while since he'd been inside it. All his *Dungeons & Dragons* posters had been replaced by bikinied women. Chuck was on his Apple IIc, playing *The Coveted Mirror.* He spun around as Seb entered. "What's the big idea?"

"Your mom let me in," Seb said. He glanced at the computer screen, depicting in glorious eight-bit graphics an old hermit wiggling his fingers. "You need to learn sign language before meeting him. Look for the priest at the tavern."

Chuck's eyes lit up. "Cool. But wait. What are you—?"

"There's no time." He strode to Chuck's bookshelf and unplugged his piggy bank.

"No, really," Chuck said, stopping Seb. "Wait."

"I need cash," Seb said.

"And I need Kim Basinger's number. What's gotten into you, Theb?"

The thought of explaining it all to Chuck seemed almost as daunting as living it again. He pulled out twenty-five dollars. "You owe me at least this much."

"I *what?*"

"*Timmy*," Seb said, "you said the name *Timmy*. That's where everything fell apart, remember?"

Chuck raised an eyebrow. "Seriously?"

"If you hadn't said—"

"Whatever, Seb. Just pay me back."

Seb stuffed the money into his pocket. "Then get your pilot's cap on and come with."

He grabbed Chuck's arm and pulled him downstairs, then through his house to his garage. Chuck's look of perplexity gave way to guilt. "Um, Seb, I have to..."

"Not now." Seb climbed about Chuck's sister's bike. It was purple with rainbow streamers, but it'd do. "Tell me when we get there."

"Where?"

Seb pedaled down the driveway. "The flying fields," he called behind. "I'm buying the Dreamin' tonight."

*   *   *   *   *

The flying fields of Stony Glen raced to each of the four horizons. An unknowing visitor could be forgiven for believing, momentarily, he'd strayed into eastern Montana or Kansas. Once upon a time, the town had figured prominently in American aviation. But time and the march of progress had gutted Stony Glen of its soul, leaving only hollow husks of what had been a glorious past. The hulk of the flyers' eatery, shaped like a bulbous dirigible, built when theme diners had been all the rage, was the only landmark in the drab panorama. Chuck said, "Do you think those pilots had any idea?"

"Huh?" Seb said. He was focused on Timmy, who was running late.

"I mean, one minute they're eating inside a zeppelin, the next they're at war with the Germans who built them."

Chuck pondered the strangest things. Seb said, "No."

"What do you think Lloyd Llewellyn would think."

"About what?

Chuck said, "Things. Nights like this. What became of his old stomping-grounds, and what became of his friends."

Friends? No friend had stood up for Seb against Rob and Aloysius. No friend had helped him earn three hundred dollars. He, himself, was the only reason his odyssey was culminating here. "He didn't need friends," Seb said. "All he did, he did alone." Chuck looked askance. A flock of pigeons trundled past, a lambent constellation. Seb said, "So what was it you wanted to tell me?"

Chuck said, "Oh, yeah." He licked his lips. "Well—"

A high-pitched whine, like a mutant hornet, rose above the field. The pigeons scattered. Seb looked up. A tiny blur of red and beige zipped from west to east.

It was the Dreamin'. And it was flying awfully fast—and high.

"Hey, faggot!" Timmy stepped from the corn at the flying field's edge, radio controller slung from his neck. He took his hands off the controls. The Dreamin' rattled downwards.

Chuck waved his arms. "Don't!"

"Oops," Timmy said. "Silly me. But how can you blame me? My arms are tired from working all day, alone. See, I had this employee, but he fucked me over. What's a businessman to do?" He jammed his thumbs on the servo-sticks. The Dreamin' throttled back into flight.

Seb should have known Timmy would pull such a stunt. Why else would he have insisted on making the exchange here? But Timmy would never crash the Dreamin'. He'd get no cash and his brothers would kill him. Seb said, "Land the plane."

"No can do," Timmy said. "Never learned." He throttled it sharply downwards. "I guess I could try—"

Chuck cried, "No!"

"Don't sweat it," Seb said. "He's screwing with me."

Timmy pulled the Dreamin' out of the dive. "I wonder what her top speed is. *Maverick, this is Iceman. I've got bogies on my tail.*" He eased the sticks forward. The Dreamin' sped off into the distance, all but grazing the tops of the trees that lined the southern edge of the field.

"I can't watch," Chuck said.

Seb didn't budge: Timmy had to be bluffing. Not even Timmy could be so self-destructive. But the quicker the purchase, the better. "Here." He pulled the money out of his pocket. "Put the radio around Chuck's neck. Then you'll get your cash."

Timmy laughed. "Hand it over first, bozo, then I'll put it on your girlfriend's neck."

"Boyfriend," Chuck said. "He's the girl."

"Got that right," Timmy said. He jammed the servo-sticks hard outboard. The Dreamin' wheeled into a spin.

Seb crossed his arms. He'd seen enough Timmy the past six weeks to know what his endgame was. "You win, Mr. Vaughn," Seb said. "I should never have taken that tip from Osur. We had a good thing going, and I ruined it. Happy?"

"Surprisingly, yes," Timmy said. He banked the Dreamin' into a turn and looped it back across the field. "But something here has gotta give. And it's going to be you."

Chuck said, "Do it, Seb. Enough Sicilian mind-games."

Seb stood firm. He had one bargaining chip.

Timmy yanked the plane to a climb, humming the theme from *Jeopardy.* "Doo doo *doo,* do do doo doo *doo...*"

Chuck grabbed his arm. "Seb!"

"No."

Timmy eased the throttle. "Tsk, tsk, tsk, only a drip of gasoline left, just like Amelia Earhart. If you're not going to buy it, I'll have to head home." He took a few strides up the road.

Checkmate. Whether or not Seb trusted him, there was nothing forcing Timmy to sell. His window was closing. There was too much at stake. "All right, wait," Seb said.

Timmy stopped. "Yes, ma'am?"

Seb squeezed the wad of money, still moist with the sweat of six weeks' hard labor, then slapped it into Timmy's hand. "Done," he said. "Hand it over."

A car engine growled, drawing near. A Chevy sports van, complete with elk roof and opaque windows, sped towards them over the hill, kicking up clouds of dust as it came. Seb recognized the vehicle, its driver, and passenger. It was Timmy's two brothers, Eddie and Ted.

"Right on time," Timmy said. The van pulled to a halt. "You guys ready for the movie?"

Eddie and Ted gave grinning thumbs-ups.

Seb had been had. "What movie?" he said.

Timmy jammed the servo-sticks forward. "*Airport 1975.*"

The Dreamin' screamed its loudest note, then droned to its highest apex. Seb lunged at Timmy, grabbing pell-mell; reaching for either the money or radio, or neither, or both, with the very same hand. "No," Seb said. "Don't do it. No!"

Timmy coolly dodged each swipe. "Mayday!" he wailed, "Mayday! To the tower. The tower! We're going down! Mayday!"

He pulled the radio off his neck and held it high above his head. The Dreamin' fell silent, then plummeted. Seb reached for the radio. Timmy shoved him.

"Mayday!"

Seb fell to his knees. Chuck ran to his side. They could only look on in horror.

"*Mayday—*"

The Dreamin' slammed against the ground in a shower of balsa, metal, and plastic. "That's how the movie ended, right?" Timmy said. "I never saw the whole thing through.

It was always on way past my bedtime." He flung the radio into the air. It, too, struck the pavement and shattered.

Timmy climbed into the van. "So long, sucker. Don't let me hear you're running your mouth." The van peeled away in a cloud of black dust.

Seb knelt above the ruined Dreamin' as Chuck retrieved what was left of the radio. The direct impact, at full speed, had split the engine and broken all beams. It was even worse-off than his father's had been; clearly irreparable, barely recognizable. "Damn it," Seb said. It was like a recurrent nightmare.

Chuck set the husk of radio down. "What are you going to do now?"

A riptide of thoughts swirled about in Seb's brain. There was no point going to Mr. Sweeny now: he couldn't get Seb's money back. Timmy would only deny cheating, then pound Seb senseless the first chance he got. Timmy's mother and father would side with their son, and Seb's parents had their own problems. Telling them could make things worse, especially if they found out how he'd made so much money so quickly. "Nothing," Seb said.

"Nothing?"

"Is there an echo?"

"Well, I'd do something, or you paid three hundred dollars for scrap."

Chuck's rare gift for stating the obvious grated on Seb's last nerve. "So helpful," Seb said. "This saves you from having to teach me, I guess."

Chuck looked down at his feet. "Yeah, about that."

Seb recognized that tone of voice. Bad news loomed. "What?"

Chuck kicked a stone. "Well, I...I need to, um...clarify."

"Clarify what?"

"I'm not technically an R/C pilot."

The words hit like a wrecking-ball. "What?"

Chuck's face brightened. "I have flown R/C planes, though."

It was all happening much too fast. And he could tell Chuck was still holding back. "You've flown R/C planes?"

"Absolutely," Chuck replied. Then, softer, he said, "Once."

"Come again?"

"I flew my friend's once."

"What?"

"I flew my friend's once."

Seb closed his eyes, not believing his ears. "That's it? You flew your friend's once?"

"Yes—er, well..."

What more could there be? "Well, what?"

Chuck fidgeted with his shirttails. "Well, to be exact, I, um...I, um...I sort of just watched him fly it. Once." His face brightened again. "But I'm sure I could remember."

Seb gathered the shards of the Dreamin'. Not only was it garbage now, he couldn't have piloted it, anyway. He laughed aloud, cynically. Chuck, for reasons known only to him, had bluffed him into a sense of surety. Timmy had probably planned his betrayal. Seb's whole quest had been based on lies. "Great," he said. "Could this get any worse?"

The screech of familiar bald tires rang out. Seb looked up the road. From the same direction the Vaughns' van had come, his mother's Gremlin appeared. From its speed he could tell that whatever was happening, he'd be ruing it for a very long time.

"I guess so," Chuck said.

The car shrieked to a stop. Seb's father stormed from the passenger seat, and in the sternest voice imaginable said, "Did you steal Mr. Vincenti's string-trimmer?"

Chuck looked at Seb. "Steal?"

Seb's life was unraveling at breakneck speed. "Wait—"

"Answer me!" his father said.

"Um..." he hemmed, but the jig was up. There was no use stalling. He nodded, "Yes."

Rich's eyes spread like searchlights. "Where is it?"

"*I* lost it," Chuck said.

But Seb had had it with Chuck and his fibs, even if he was trying to help. "No," Seb said, "I lost it."

"Get in the car," Diane said. "Both of you ought to know better." Chuck mounted his bike and pedaled away, leading his sister's bike like a pony. Seb watched him trundle up the road, coughing in the cloud of dust kicked up by the Vaughns' barnstorming van. He bent to gather the shards of the Dreamin'. "Now!" his mother screamed.

He slunk in the back seat and buckled his seat belt. The upholstery was hot, and rough. Kit, beside him, whispered, "I'm sorry."

He was in no mood. "Right," he grumbled, "as if you cared. All you want's your stupid dog." She held a lingering stare his way, then turned aside, eyes tearing up.

The Gremlin sputtered up the road. Seb clasped the winder to roll down the window, but quickly thought the better of it. His father said, "How much did you pay that kid for that plane?"

As if it made a difference now. "Three hundred," Seb replied.

"Three hundred dollars," his father said. "Think if you'd done something worthwhile with it. We might have been able to get the roof fixed. We might even be going to Ocean City. But now, we can't afford even that."

A rage took flame in the pit of Seb's belly, growing with every moment that passed. His father had insulted him, then sold off a fixable airplane for scrap. His mother had washed her hands of it all. Timmy had tried to blackmail him, and he'd only escaped it by threatening in kind. The string-trimmer, not to mention his bike, had been stolen.

The Dreamin' he'd earned had been stolen, then wrecked. *He* was the victim here. "But dad—"

"Save it. I'm ashamed of you."

"You're paying Larry back," Diane said, "every last god-dam penny. I don't care how broke we are, I'm not raising a thief. I don't care if it takes all summer."

But summer was already half-over, the cicadas well into their first matinees. Short of hitting the lottery or knocking over a convenience store, his prospects at making another three hundred dollars, on top of what he'd have to pay Larry, were infinitesimally small. Chuck, Rob, Aloysius, Timmy, and now his parents had fucked him. The *world* had fucked him. He owed each of them a little something. Batman would have felt the same.

"Tomorrow, you're going to Larry," Diane said. "If he calls the police, you're on your own."

Seb laid his face against the window. In the pink firmament, a jet lumbered along, bound, no doubt, for warmer climes and filled with happy passengers. Rock bottom felt strangely warm and inviting: Seb could see clearly now why some people give up and part with their dreams like wayward, escaped balloons.

But he wasn't such a person. And tomorrow—somehow, some way—he'd rise.

xïi.

THE WALK TO HIS NEIGHBOR'S HOUSE was short, but it might as well have been one thousand miles. Seb shuddered stepping onto the path that led to Ashy Larry's door. The quaint 1940's Cape Cod loomed, a medieval citadel, concealing torture and death within. But what choice did he have? Vis-à-vis his fire-spitting mother, he'd a better chance of survival here. He'd known the risk when he'd first taken it.

He steeled himself and rang the doorbell. Larry, in thick bathrobe and cap, appeared. "Hurry," he said. "You'll let the cold in."

It couldn't have been less than ninety degrees, with humidity one could cut with a knife. "Cold?"

"Quick, quick." He ushered Seb in.

The house was smelly and disheveled, as if no one had cleaned and vacuumed for months. The furniture seemed to have once been stylish, but long since worn to secondhand. Heavy glass ashtrays lay scattered about. He'd heard rumors Larry came from money, but hard times had reduced him to penury. It seemed a fitting place to die.

"Why you not just ask, Sebastian?" Larry asked. He seemed more hurt than angry. "I'd have happily let you use it for free."

The tension diffused: Seb was going to live. And yet, the words tormented. Why *hadn't* he just asked? He racked his mind a moment or two. "Trying to be cool, I guess."

"Cool," he scoffed. "*Cazzate.*"

"I'm sorry," Seb said, meaning it, though wishing more he hadn't been caught.

"Well, no despair," Larry said. "Here's where you learn who you really are. Between a rock and a hard place, Seb, then as far as your feet will carry you. That's where you'll find what matters most."

"You told me that already."

"I did? Good words. A wise man told me. Then my life was never the same." He stared blankly into the distance.

Seb waved his hand by the old man's face. "Mr. Vincenti."

"I told you. Larry."

"Larry—"

"You're no kid anymore, whatever you did. Let's see if you become a man."

Larry was zany as ever. Seb had gotten more than he bargained for the moment he decided to involve him. "How much do I need to work off?"

He pulled a receipt from his kitchen counter. "Just two hundred dollars."

Seb said, "*Just* two hundred?"

"Who you think I am, Donald Trump? October 19, 1987, Sebastian. I can't just eat two hundred bucks."

Seb was lucky Larry was this generous. Anyone else would have called the police. "How long?"

"One month," Larry said. "It'll be good for you."

He sighed. Two hundred dollars in thirty-one days. Where was he even going to start? It was too late to get work at the snack bar or caddying. He was already twenty-five dollars in hock to Chuck. And he probably had a better chance of getting hit by lightning than getting his job back from Timmy.

Timmy! That name struck fear in his heart once again, as it had six weeks ago.

A surprising image caught Seb's eye: a vintage Lockheed Vega, the workhorse Wiley Post flew around the globe twice and Amelia Earhart crossed the Atlantic in. An entire wall of Larry's den was covered with old photographs. Like a treasure trove of images from aviation's golden days, each one shined in its very own right. Seb recognized each famous airplane: Ford Trimotor, DC-3. Howard Hughes' own H-1 racer. He'd known Stony Glen had a rich history, but he'd had no idea. Chuck would've gone gaga for photos like this. "Our town in its heyday," Larry said.

Then Seb's eyes settled on one, grainy and faded, but set apart from the other pictures, as if in a place of honor. "Wait a minute." He looked closer. The photograph was that of a pilot, surrounded by his flight crew, mechanics, and airstrip personnel. The pilot was unmistakable. Seb turned to Larry. "You knew Lloyd Llewellyn?"

Larry said, "Who?"

"This one here?" Seb said, pointing. Larry looked away. "You know," Seb said, "Stony Glen's most famous man. Lafayette Escadrille, World War I. More kills than any American pilot except Rickenbacker. First man to fly above the North Pole. Distinguished Flying Cross. Croix de Guerre—"

"Old trimmer's out in the shed," Larry said. "You can use it to work off what you owe me. Same goes for all the other gear, too."

But Seb was incredulous. Larry had to be holding back. If Chuck had been here, he'd have made Larry talk. He'd have annoyed him until the old man cried uncle. "You really don't know who Lloyd Llewellyn is?"

Larry grabbed a cigar. "Make sure you mix oil into the gas."

"Are you kidding me?"

"Shed's unlocked."

There was no sense pressing. Larry, now, had been doubly generous. Two hundred bucks wasn't earning itself. Seb said, "Thanks—"

He stumbled against a folding table, sending magazines tumbling. "Sorry." He knelt to collect them. "Wait." From midway down the pile, a familiar sight peeked out. "Huh?"

He pulled the magazine. It was *R/C Modeler,* July 1989. On the cover was a photo of a sleek stunt airplane, with caption:

DREAMIN' 1990
Return of a Classic
On Sale thru August 31

Was he hallucinating?

"My grandkids buy that trash," Larry said, "then leave it lying around."

Seb stared in rapt silence. The Dreamin' 1990. From the looks of it, it was smaller than the original, but battery-powered and Styrofoam. He asked, "Could you part with this one?"

Larry waved his hand. "Take 'em all."

Seb collected the modeler mags, then turned to the one he'd noticed first. He flipped to the full advertisement. Beneath a photo of the new Dreamin', red, white, and gold, with checkerboard wings, the text read in bold:

A Blast from the Past for a New Decade
$299.95 through August 31
This is NOT Your Father's Dreamin'!

The irony. If he'd been more careful with his father's Dreamin', he wouldn't be reading this magazine. And two hundred and ninety-nine dollars, ninety-five cents? He whispered to himself, "A whole nickel. Wow."

Larry said, "What?"

"Oh, nothing," Seb said. And yet...

He perused the specifications. As he'd suspected, it was an Almost-Ready-to-Fly, what modelers called an "Arf." No construction would be necessary. Save for an overnight battery-charge, it'd be good to fly right out of the box.

"You want a drink, Sebastian," Larry said. "RC Cola, maybe?"

Seb wanted R/C-*something*, but it was no drink. "I'm good," he said. But he wasn't. And yet...

It was only July 29th. The summer was half-over, yes, but half of it remained. As the yin to his former employer's yang, he'd gotten to know the customers well; they often waved to him downtown, reminding him, huffily, they were overdue for yardwork. He was no green thumb, but with hard work and a little luck, he could hold his own.

He looked back at the magazine. The Dreamin' was on sale through August 31st, which gave him just about five weeks. He had to earn two hundred dollars for Larry, but no one said he had to stop there—

But no! There was still that scourge of everything good and decent and pure in the world, and it went by the name of Timmy. Unless...

It was worth a try. The worst that could happen was that he'd fail, and by now he was used to that.

"Mr. Larry?" He drew a fluttering, anxious breath. "About what you said before..."

xiii.

SEB SCRAMBLED pell-mell along Dunbar Drive, a stack of fliers wedged under his arm, a stapler in his hand. He lurched to a stop at a telephone pole, ripped off the fliers already there, and replaced them with his fresh-printed broadsides. One of the fliers slipped from his pile and floated away on the late-July breeze. It was just as well, like dropping leaflets behind enemy lines. There was no such thing as bad publicity—except, he'd once heard, one's obituary. And he had a new lease on life today. What he was about to create would be epic.

Seb, Inc.

He tingled all over. What a name! What a concept! And it, plus a little elbow grease, would deliver the Dreamin' inside the month.

Larry had actually meant what he'd said. As long as Seb provided gas and upkeep, he could use Larry's equipment as much as he needed. Whatever landscaping services Timmy offered, Seb could do them just as well, for less. His secret? The best volunteer workforce this side of a prison. They were going to get him across the finish. They just didn't know it yet.

He rounded the corner yards from his house. A man in a tool belt was walking down his driveway, with Rich in hasty pursuit, imploring, "Please, you know I'm good for it."

The man climbed into a contractor van, parked across the street. "Riggs," he said, "that's the best I can do. The job's bigger than it looks."

"I already started it," Rich said. "It just needs a finishing touch."

He laughed. "That's what you call frame, sheetrock, and roofing? Even with the tarp, that wood's a mess. It's a full rebuild, in my opinion. One thousand down, and that's a bargain."

Rich's glance settled on Seb, approaching. "I don't have one thousand dollars." He stared at the fliers in Seb's hands.

"Well, there's time," the builder said, starting the van's engine. "Still two months of balmy air before the October chill. Of course, if there's an early snow..." He pulled into the street.

Seb looked at the flapping ceiling-tarp, then back at his father. His hand looked splotched and ugly. Rich pulled it behind his back. "Freeloader," he said.

"The nerve," Seb said, "trying to fleece you."

"I wasn't talking about *him*," Rich said, and strode back towards the house.

In normal times, the words would have hurt. But these were anything but normal. It was only Rich's desperation talking: Seb comforted himself with that. A golden world was dawning fast. He was about to embark on an audacious venture.

He ran from the street into his backyard. As he'd requested, Chuck and Kit were waiting. He cleared his throat, mounted a cinderblock, and in his best Convincing John from *Fraggle Rock* announced, "You're probably wondering what this is about. Well, fret no further, foot-soldiers."

Kit said, "Whose shoulders?"

"Soldiers," Chuck said. "This ought to be good."

"Oh, but it is." Seb handed them each a flier.

Chuck's eyes scanned the page, then rolled. "For real? A

lawn service? I thought this was going to be about Gypsy Pond finally."

Seb had anticipated just that reaction. "Think how cool Gypsy Pond will be when glimpsed from the air from a spy camera mounted aboard my new Dreamin' Arf." He grinned ear to ear.

Chuck wasn't biting. "Or we could just ride bikes there, like now."

"Sorry," Seb said, "but today's booked solid." At least it might be if they hurried. Seb had already made a phone call but the prospective client still needed convincing. It was a longshot but what choice did he have?

Chuck said, "Jobs already?"

"Sale ends August 31st. Dollar bills don't grow on trees."

"Seb, get with it," Chuck said. "No one can make that much money that fast, on top of what you owe Larry."

"Alone," Seb said, "you're right. But lucky for me..." He slapped Chuck's back.

Chuck shook his head dolefully. "This was supposed to be *our* summer, Seb. *Batman,* Gypsy Pond, Friday nights at the field throwing popcorn at kids making out under the bleachers. What the hell's gotten into you?"

For a moment it sounded heavenly. The halcyon days of summers past—fishing with droplines in the creek at sunup, afternoons racing dirt bikes, evenings devouring M&M's from a saucepan while playing *Star Voyager*—felt lost yet still palpable, like the light from a supernova. Life, back then, had seemed effortless; now, every day was an obstacle course. But the Dreamin' would rekindle that spark and light the way to better days. "I'll make it worth your while," Seb said.

"Oh yeah," Chuck said. "How?"

"We'll be moving mountains. And once I get the Dreamin', you'll be cool by association."

Chuck said, "Big of you, Rob. Or is it Aloysius?"

That was a low blow, and it landed. Chuck had partially created Seb's problems. The least he could do was help out. "Listen, dipstick—"

"I'll help," Kit said.

The tension dissipated. Brother and sister glowered at Chuck for what felt like a moment stretched to infinity. "Well?" Seb said. He wasn't about to hear no.

"This was a setup from jump-street," Chuck said. "Fine, this once. But I have to be home by four."

Seb ignored the caveat. "Splendid." He handed Kit the fliers and stapler. "Hang these all over the neighborhood. Get your friends to help."

"Indubitably," she said. She skipped away towards Dunbar Drive, calling for her friends. "Lisa, Tori...Seb needs us!"

It was a good enough start but the real challenge loomed. "Come with me," Seb said to Chuck.

They climbed Larry's fence and entered the shed. Seb felt inclined to hunker down, so second-nature sneaking had become. He'd have sworn, for an instant, he almost missed it: the life of an outlaw swapped for wage work. He filled the string-trimmer and lawnmower with gas, then dragged them, along with hedge-clipper and cord, out of the shed and into his driveway. Rummaging through a garage storage-nook, he located his ancient red Radio Flyer and wheeled it beside the equipment.

Chuck said, "Where are we going?"

"To vanquish a foe," Seb said. With Chuck, the key was making the bland seem heroic. "There's a chump I know who's losing his job. We're going to take it off his hands."

Chuck, seeming unimpressed, glanced at his watch. "As long as he's vanquished by three forty-five. If not, you're on your own."

They started at a hurried clip, Seb pushing the mower, Chuck dragging the wagon. Its wheels on pavement made a racket, drawing raised eyebrows from onlookers. Chuck said, "People are staring."

"Word of mouth," Seb said. "There's no better advertising."

The blocks grew longer, the sidewalks narrower, the houses less cookie-cutter and farther apart. The trees loomed thicker overhead. The trilling of warblers and cawing of crows replaced the mewling of neighborhood kids and chides of exasperated parents. Chuck, behind him, made no sound. Seb, once or twice, thought of making small-talk, then realized he had nothing to say. Six weeks of putting distance between he and Chuck had borne its bitter fruit. But he'd never considered he'd be tasting it, too.

The sidewalk ended, the oaks closed ranks. A dirt path wended off the road, then into a glade with a brown clapboard shack. A nearby sign read:

Lorrimer Wood

Seb said, "We're here."

Past the shack, on the left, the trees rose higher; to the right, they dropped in favor of hedgerows and rolling expanses of motley-hued flowers. In the distance, atop a twenty-foot pole, stood a Victorian purple martin house. The air was filled with the droning of sweat bees and tiny, bejeweled hummingbirds. "The sanctuary?" Chuck said.

"String-trimmer's paradise," Seb said. "I hope you're not allergic to poison ivy."

He winced. "What if I am?"

"Wear sleeves next time."

"*Next* time—?"

"You again, faggot?"

They turned. It was Timmy.

He was standing beside the clapboard shack, unloading

landscaping tools from his cart. Judging by the shiner on his left eye, someone had taken exception to him since the last time they'd crossed paths.

Chuck trembled. "That's the chump?"

"Have faith," Seb said. The sanctuary was Timmy's oldest client; Seb knew he'd been bilking it for years. He hadn't expected what he'd been planning would happen in real time, before Timmy's eyes. This would be sweeter than he'd ever dreamed—at least, he prayed it would.

"Hit the road," Timmy said. "Take your girlfriend to see *When Harry Met Sally.*"

Seb ignored him. He strode to the door and knocked. "Mr. Schultz?"

Timmy reared up. "What part of hit the road did you not understand?"

"We're birdwatching," Chuck said.

"That's right," Seb said. "Came to see the dodo."

"You're a long way from Mauritius." Timmy reached for his fly. "But I can show you a woodpecker—"

"Can I help you?" Mr. Schultz, the manager, said. Seb knew him from around Stony Glen, always with field-glasses slung round his neck and driving a beat-up Mercedes-Benz.

"Mr. Schultz," Seb said, "I'm Sebastian, the one who called earlier."

"Hmm," the owlish birdwatcher said. "Didn't I say I wasn't interested?"

Timmy harrumphed, "Straight up."

Seb scrutinized his surroundings, suddenly glad he'd studied field guides while the rest of his classmates were playing with He-Man. "I love the purple martin house. And did I notice a couple of Karner blue butterflies darting among the wild lupine?"

Schultz cracked a smirk. "Promising."

"Gag me with a spoon," Timmy said. "Money talks."

"Exactly," Seb said, "So right to the point." There'd be

no going back once he threw down the gauntlet. "Whatever Timmy's charging you, cut it in half."

A cardinal crooned, a house sparrow peeped. A pointed, pregnant silence fell, punctuated by Schultz and Timmy chuckling, one in surprise, the other contempt. Even Chuck let slip a dribble of doubt and said, "You must be joking."

Seb said, "Do I look like I'm joking?"

Schultz stopped laughing. "Seriously?"

"Fun, fun," Timmy said, "but now playtime's over. Time for your afternoon naps, buckaroos." He bent to unfasten the mower's hitch-ball.

Seb stood firm. "You heard me. Half."

Doubt and intrigue took turns on Schultz's face. "He charges me eighty dollars."

"Then I'll do it for forty and take less time."

"It takes as long as it takes," Timmy said. "You can't promise something like that."

"Watch me," Seb said. "Four hours, forty bucks."

Chuck drew closer. "Remember, I told you, three forty-five—"

"*Quiet*. What do you think, Mr. Schultz?"

He mulled in silence. "I think maybe you haven't thought this through. But that's your problem, not mine. Not yet."

Seb was reeling his first catch in. Timmy, for once, was tasting crow. It all felt so sublime.

"All right," Timmy said, a hint of worry in his voice, "if this is how it's gonna be. I'll knock fifteen dollars off. That's sixty-five bucks and you know what you're getting."

Seb pictured the beautiful Dreamin' in pieces. "Thirty-five," he shot back. "You have nothing to lose."

Chuck tugged on his shirt. "Seb?"

"Shut it. Thirty-five bucks, and we'll be here each Wednesday."

Mr. Schultz said, "Well, that *is* tempting."

"That's a pig in a poke," Timmy said. "This homo used to work for me. He's a dimwit on a good day, not to mention a cheat and a liar."

True, Seb *had been* a cheat and a liar. The tongue-lashing he'd had at the hands of his parents had left scars only time would heal. But he'd only been hardened by the experience. And like a starving wolverine, calling quits now could only mean death. "All right, *thirty.*"

Chuck squeaked, "What?" Timmy's jaw trundled wide. Schultz just stared with furrowed brow.

"Judge for yourself, Mr. Schultz," Seb said. "Give me a chance. It's no skin off your back."

Timmy said, "Listen, faggot, it's called economics. You can't work even *half* a day, buy gasoline, maintain your gear, pay a worker, and expect to walk away with profit. You might as well just volunteer."

Schultz nodded. "I have to agree. Even at that price, it's a shot in the dark. I'd go home and rethink this." He adjusted his glasses.

"Wait," Seb said. He drew a deep breath. He'd anticipated everything correctly so far. It was time for the coup de grâce. He'd held onto the ace up his sleeve just for this. He steeled himself and whispered to Chuck, "You don't really care if you get paid, do you?"

Chuck stammered, "Well...I—"

"I'll do the whole job for just twenty-five bucks. The hedges, butterfly gardens, and trails." He glimpsed Schultz's antediluvian Benz, coated with guano and dust. "And I'll wash your car for free."

Timmy staggered, as if shot in the head. "I can't match that!"

Schultz said, "Can't or won't?"

"Can't *and* won't. No one can do it that cheap and promise quality. This weasel doesn't know crap about shit, and he thinks you're stupid."

"Language, language," Schultz scolded. "Those Karner blues can pick up bad vibes."

"And I can pick up bullshit," Timmy said, "apparently better than you. Have I let you down once in two years?"

Mr. Schultz scowled. "Well..."

"Don't answer that. But why change horses in mid-stream?"

"What was it you told me?" Seb said. "That time is money, so slow it down... we want to milk these suckers?"

Mr. Schultz glowered at Timmy. "Well, that explains quite a bit."

"Fucking cum-stain," Timmy snarled.

Chuck said, "Seb, are you insane?"

"We'll settle up later," Seb said. "Play along."

"You've gone bye-bye, Seb."

But Seb, as he hadn't in quite a long time, was feeling every inch of his oats. He reached out his hand for Mr. Schultz's. "So, we have a deal?"

Schultz hesitated, then clasped Seb's hand. "Yes, I believe we do." His grip was like a slippery fish, but at this point, who cared? Seb, Inc. was officially off the ground. "My regrets, Timmy. Business is business."

"Said the man who watches birds," Timmy said, sounding strangely Zen. "But I know how this is going to end. Just don't call my house too late. My mother likes her beauty sleep." He gathered his gear and loaded his cart. At length, he turned to Seb. "Remember Saturday morning cartoons?"

He could hardly imagine a less relevant question. "I do."

"Well," Timmy said, "when the coyote finally caught the roadrunner, what was left for him to do?"

Timmy, Seb had to admit yet again, was so much smarter than anyone gave him credit for. As furious as Seb was over the Dreamin', he couldn't find hate anywhere in his heart. Yet, nor could he grasp the ominous warning. Timmy knew something he wasn't letting on. Timmy, maybe even, had ghosts of his own. Seb said, "I don't get it."

"You will," Timmy said. "For now, lots of luck." He motored his golf cart down the dirt path and disappeared behind the trees.

"Bucket and soap are out back," Schultz said. "Don't make me regret this." He stepped into the shack. Its rickety door slammed shut behind him.

Somewhere in the boughs overhead, a Baltimore oriole chattered away. Closer to where Mr. Schultz had been standing, a furtive chipmunk scuttled past. Seb stared at Chuck and Chuck stared back. It was hard to tell who was more surprised. This all had been done on a wing and a prayer. Where, exactly, had he gone right? Triumph, it seemed, vexed as much as failure.

But because of or in spite of himself, Seb, Inc. now was real. "Um," he said, "follow me, I guess." He plugged the extension cord into an outlet, then wheeled the wagon to the base of the hedgerow. It loomed above like a menacing dyke: thorny, green, and buzzing with bees. "All yours, big guy. I'll be off trimming trails. Mind the Dobson flies at dusk."

Chuck said, "I have to be home by four, remember?"

Always, always was Chuck with his snivels. But Seb had promises to keep. "Make it five and let's get cracking."

"But I told you—"

"You owe me." Chuck had worn Seb's patience threadbare. He'd have long since mastered his father's Dreamin' had Chuck not been so recklessly dumb that evening in June. "I don't have time to list all the reasons." He lifted Larry's electric hedge clipper and shoved it hard against Chuck's chest. "Cut the cord and I cut your dick, assuming I could find it."

Chuck's eyes swelled red. He took the clippers. Then he turned his back to Seb, and set to gnawing away at the bush.

Seb grabbed the string-trimmer and marched to the trailhead. And as he did, he thought about Timmy. "Fucking wheel of commerce," he said. "Let's go make that omelet."

xiv.

AUGUST IS A GOLDEN CROWN upon the brow of summer. August is Hi-C, katydid songs, and tall sunflowers in manicured gardens. August is lazy days at the beach, neon-bright boardwalk nights, and wee morning hours in loving embraces awaiting ruddy sunrises. August is sleep-away camp in the hills, polar bear swims and flag football games, and long, ghostly yarns beside campfires, nibbling gooey s'mores. August is the Perseid meteor shower, back-to-school sales, and grandiose weddings played out in pavilions decked with gladiolas. August is the last of the bum-lazy days, so splendid in their emptiness, so idle in their passage, yet tinged with bittersweet surrender to the seasons' indelible march.

But August for Seb was a time to reap. Without his meaning, much less even knowing, the seeds he'd planted in July had blossomed into his own money tree. Yet, the thing, as he learned, about money trees is just how hard they are to prune. Having thought he'd known hard work before, each day brought another grueling lesson that, really, he'd been clueless. From sunup to sunset and all in between, from sprawling estates up Woodmansee Hill to postage-stamp duplexes down in the hollow, from simple "eh, just cut the grass" to intricate "I'm hoping Robin Leach notices," the gamut of toil was excruciating. Chuck and Kit continued to help: more than they'd have liked, he was sure, but he'd wheedled, cajoled, and coaxed zealously, and when that didn't work, there were always guilt-trips.

So the money began to pile up, as did expenses and wear on the gear. Gasoline, oil, and clippings-bags gorged on his gains. But he persisted, and rolled with the punches, and in no time his profits began to expand.

Which was a good thing, for so did his dreams, and so did his reveries of flight. Even optimistically, there was next to no chance he'd have the Dreamin' before Labor Day, but there'd still be three weeks of summer and fair weather well into November. The details of his plans had changed, even if its grandeur hadn't. Saturday of the first week of school, he'd still take off atop the Hill, except, this time, there'd be no Chuck, just Seb alone at the stick. He'd throttle the Dreamin' above the mansions, taking pains to ensure he buzzed Timmy's window, the aviation equivalent of a fat middle finger. Then he'd wheel the Dreamin' south, above the glen to the downtown, striding like a brash conqueror as reams of children thronged his coattails. And then, in a final, glorious flourish, he'd land the Dreamin' on the school soccer field, in the middle of Lauren's practice or game, then gather her, swooning, into his arms, and—

"Seb!"

The reverie shattered. Seb opened his eyes. Chuck, straining beneath a clippings-bag, shouted from across the yard, "You wanna give me a hand with this, boss?"

Lauren's lips disappeared in the ether. Seb shook off the cobwebs, swigging ice-water. "Looks like you're doing just fine."

Chuck said, "I wasn't *asking*—"

"I'm here!" Kit came running up the driveway, disheveled and covered with what looked like cat fur, eyes puffy red. "Sorry I'm late."

It was about damn time, too. "Well, well," Seb said, "she finally shows up. Where the heck have you been, anyway?"

She blew him a raspberry. "I'll never tell." She plunged a rake into the clippings-pile as Chuck hauled his bag to the curb.

Seb downed another icy draught and surveyed Mr. Osur's yard, the latest fiefdom in his growing empire. He'd come astoundingly far in two weeks. Owlish old Schultz had been effusive, and word of mouth had spread like wildfire. From one end of Stony Glen to the other, homeowners and businesses alike were eager to shuffle out from under Timmy and cast their lot with the new upstart. Seb's client list was expanding geometrically. There was no way he could keep this pace: sooner or later, he'd forfeit quality. But by then it wouldn't matter because by then he'd have the Dreamin'.

Chuck came up beside him. "How 'bout cutting her some slack?"

Seb looked at his sister, feverishly filling another bag. "We're fifty bucks short of paying off Larry."

Chuck said, "*We're?*"

"All for one," Seb said. He relished watching the sylph princess toiling. "I'm her big brother. You know the perks."

"Bullcrap," Chuck snapped, a rusty edge to his voice.

"Why don't you take a five-minute break?"

"Why don't you help us?"

"Okay, ten minutes."

"Get off your ass, Seb. *We're* exhausted."

Seb said, "I'm allowed a breather. I've been working just as hard as you. And when we're done here, I have more jobs I'm doing, *alone,* not to mention buying gas and cleaning. So don't act like I'm treating you like slaves." He popped in his earplugs.

Chuck tugged Seb's shirt-tail and said, "I ain't done talking." Kit froze. It wasn't like Chuck to use the word *ain't.* "I've had it with your attitude."

Seb said, "And I with yours."

"This is bullshit, Seb. When are we going to find Gypsy Pond?"

"For the hundredth time," Seb groaned, "soon enough."

"Right," Chuck said, "like *Batman*."

"You jumped the gun."

"You disappeared. How long was I supposed to wait?"

"Yeah, it must be tough," Seb said. "Hangin' loose at the pool each day."

"Play is the work of children," Chuck said. "That's what my grandfather says. Cherish your summer. Don't waste it working before you have to."

"Good for him," Seb said, "but you volunteered."

"I was volun-*told*."

"Now who's spouting bullshit, Chuck?"

"Please stop yelling," Kit said.

"Nobody's yelling," Seb said. "Keep working."

Chuck said, "Why? For peanuts, on credit?"

Seb thought he'd made it clear. "Let me spell this out, again. I have to make five hundred bucks as fast as possible. After that, I could care less. You two can split whatever profit." Truth be told, at five hundred dollars, Seb, Inc. was going to be shuttered. But Chuck and Kit didn't need to know that. "Friends help each other out," Seb said, "and best friends help each other best. Remember I fixed your aquarium filter? Or how about when I gave you five dollars for the Scholastic book fair?"

"Those were favors," Chuck said. "This is drudgery."

Kit echoed, "Sure is."

"Can it, Kathryn," Seb said. "What's it matter anyway? It's not like you've something better to do."

"I do too," Chuck said.

Seb said, "Give me three examples, besides lounging on your pampered ass, eating freeze pops, and jerking off. Really, you should thank me."

"For making me your servant?"

"For making you productive."

Kit sobbed, "Please."

"I told you," Seb barked, "shut your face. Back to work." He could feel a reservoir of rage churning deep inside. But he couldn't give in—not yet. He needed Chuck's help. There was too much at stake.

The Dreamin'. He concentrated on the Dreamin', its red and gold checkerboard-pattern wings glistening in the midday sun, looping above the soccer field, firing the flames of Lauren's wonder. It was his North Star, his true love, his purpose, his dream. He'd come too far to be denied. "Look, Chuck, this airplane... it's everything. Once I get it—"

"You'll be a kid with an R/C plane, Seb. What, you think Aloysius and Rob won't still beat you up? You think Timmy's going to give a crap, or Lauren's going to notice? You think your dad's gonna kiss your ass because you can fly some Styrofoam Arf? Wake the fuck up, Seb. Nobody cares."

The anger swelled and swirled within, a noxious witch's-brew. It spread from his chest across his limbs. It trickled along his tongue, to his lips. Chuck owed him. Dammit, Chuck owed him. "Whether or not you want to hear it, dipstick, you're a part of this—"

"No. No, Seb—just *no*. No! It's not my fault you broke your dad's model. It's not my fault Timmy swindled you. It's not my fault you stole Larry's stuff, and it sure as shit isn't my fault you turned into such a wimp-ass pussy the minute you mangled your father's hand."

Game over. The hatred broke free. He contemplated his weaponized words, then drove the shank deep into Chuck's neck. "Good thing my best friend's such a candy-ass faggot. He thinks he's going to get some someday. That's why he'll never break his leash."

Chuck crumbled, visibly. Seb had finally slain him cold.

"Oh my God!" Kit cried. "Say you're sorry!"

But he wasn't. And he wouldn't.

Chuck, through quivering voice, replied, "I'd rather be gay than be you, Seb. I know who I am, and it's enough."

"Enough, enough," came a garbled old voice. Mr. Osur opened his door. "This is my home, not a saloon." He stepped onto his wraparound porch and held out a packet of cash. "Take that gutter-talk somewhere else. My poor wife's turning in her grave."

Seb took the payment and counted it. "This is only twenty bucks."

"That's right."

Seb could see cash left in the old man's hand. Osur still had a soldier's bearing, but here he was out of his depth. And Seb could take him down if need be. He stepped in closer. "Not good enough."

Osur chuckled and undid his collar. He pulled his undershirt aside, revealing a keloid of rubbery flesh. "A love-kiss from Hitler at Bastogne. I was maybe a few years older than you. You can go now, *Timmy*."

"I'm not Timmy."

"Could have fooled me."

"I have to pay my workers."

"Way ahead of you." He waved two twenty-dollar bills in Seb's face, then motioned for Chuck and Kit to come. Seb's erstwhile best friend shook Osur's hand, then pocketed the money. Kit, still sobbing, followed suit. "Don't bother finishing," Osur said. "I'll find a couple of Mexicans. At least they won't be running their mouths." He slammed the door behind him.

Seb smarted. The bloom was finally off the rose: fired by his first customer, and a wealthy one, to boot. It had all been eerily similar to the scene three weeks ago. But Seb, Inc. was still stratosphere-bound, even if knocked off course slightly. And now, seeing life through green-colored glasses, maybe being like Timmy was a good thing. Maybe Timmy, weeks ago, had been right, and Seb had deserved to be fired.

But Chuck. *Chuck*. The name rhymed with the expletive he couldn't seem to chase from his mind. Who the hell was Chuck to complain? Whether or not Chuck wanted to hear, everything Seb had said was true—more or less, from a certain angle, depending on how you looked at it. Seb had been busting his own ass for weeks; the least Chuck could do was pitch in a little. Poor choice of insults notwithstanding, Seb's conscience was clear, and rightly so.

Wasn't it?

Seb snarled, "Benedict Arnold."

"If not for Benedict Arnold," Chuck said, "we'd all be sipping tea about now." He mounted his bike. "I hope you find what you're looking for, Seb."

Oh, but he would. "Second weekend in September," Seb said. "Look skyward. You'll see."

Chuck said, "It's sad you think that's what I meant." He trundled down the driveway.

A knot of robins dropped from the trees, hunting for earthworms in the freshly-mowed lawn and chirping gleefully. A soft breeze tussled Seb's sweaty hair, still born of air warmed by summer sun, but carrying the promise of fall in its wings. Someday soon the Dreamin' would soar, perhaps riding that very same zephyr, an updraft to eternal glory. Or else—

No. The die had been cast.

Kit said, "Now what?"

Onwards and upwards. Seb downed what was left of his ice-water, then wiped his brow of clippings-dust. "We're off to Mrs. Phillips'."

"But you said this was my only job today."

"You can thank Chuck. He ratfucked us both." He piled his equipment into the wagon, then dropped the handle at

Kit's feet. She dutifully knelt and picked it up, and dragged it down the driveway.

Seb leaned into the heavy lawnmower, heaving it along the grass and out into the roadway. The Phillips house was not far off, just a fifteen-minute walk. There were appointments to keep, customers to please, and twenty-dollar bills to harvest. Chuck and Osur were human sacrifices on the altar of the Dreamin', roadkill on the thoroughfare that led to superstardom. In the end, all they were were more broken eggs. And as he strode from Osur's house, he whistled shamelessly.

XV.

IT WAS A DARK and stormy evening. Seb secured the
landscaping equipment inside Larry's shed, then ran
through the rain to the old man's back porch. Through
the fence he could see his own house's back window. His
father was standing there, watching him.

"Mr. Vincenti?" He knocked his secret knock on the
door. It creaked ajar. It wasn't like Larry not to lock up.

He called inside, "Hello?" The house was altogether still,
save for a faint glow inside the hall. "Mr. Vin—er, Larry?
Can I come in? I have your two hundred dollars."

Silence.

The cash in his hand felt unusually weighty. Seb's goal
was tantalizingly close. He did, after all, have two weeks
left. He could buy the Dreamin' once he hit three hundred
dollars, taking the chance he'd make two hundred more
before the month was out.

No—but it was tempting. Larry had gone above and
beyond; anyone else would have pressed charges. His
mother would probably murder him if she learned he'd put
repaying Larry off. And Seb, Inc. was well on course to make
three hundred dollars by August 31st. Wasn't it?

Tempting, indeed. Better to get this over with now.

He nudged the door and slipped inside. Larry, by now,

ought to have trusted him. Outside, a crack of thunder pealed. Seb said, "Anyone home?" A faint groan rose from down the hallway. Seb counted twenty ten-dollar bills and wedged them under the dining-room centerpiece. "I left your money on—"

"*Why?*"

An icy shudder singed Seb's spine. It was Larry's voice, no doubt, but sounded more like the wail of a ghost. "Why?" it came again, "*Why?*"

Seb gathered his wits. "Because I owe you. Larry?"

A shaft of lightning rent the sky. Rain pelted the roof like incoming flak. Above the din came Larry's voice, softly, "Cold, so cold. Is that you, Brent?"

Seb crept down the hallway, towards Larry's voice. The floorboards creaked underfoot where he stepped. Past the door at the end of the hall a meager light was flickering. The air throbbed like a tropical greenhouse. The sputtering light limned the thermostat. It read eighty-seven degrees.

Seb gently pried the door. "Larry?"

The stench of mildew mixed with ash assaulted Seb's nose. Larry was laying on top of his bed, twisted and swathed in a thick mound of blankets and wrapped in his usual heavy bathrobe. His face and arms were dripping with sweat. A bedside candle lit the room, its light dancing in the sputtering gusts from Larry as he tossed. "Larry," Seb said, "it's me."

The old man's eyes stayed closed. "Brent?"

"No," he said, "Sebastian—"

He gasped. Larry's left foot was missing two toes.

Larry mumbled, "I can't see you, Brent." He writhed side-to-side and every which way until he was smothered inside his blankets.

Larry was deep in the throes of a nightmare. One errant flail of the old man's arm and the whole house would burn, with Larry inside. Seb drew breath to blow out the candle—

He stopped. On the floor was an old scrapbook. And staring up from its yellowed pages was the distinct profile of Lloyd Llewellyn.

"Brent," Larry muttered, "come back..."

Seb knelt and lifted the photograph. Other than missing its top-right corner, which appeared to have been ripped away, it was amazingly lucid. In the center was indeed Llewellyn, but gaunt and haggard-looking. Flanking him were two young males, looking about Seb's own age. One of them had bold, swarthy features. It was unmistakably Larry.

"Where are you? Brent..."

In the candlelight, Seb could see indentations. There was handwriting on the back of the photo. He flipped the picture, squinted, and read, "Larry, when I reach Valhalla, all my treasure belongs to you. Capt. L., 1936. What really matters—"

It ended abruptly. The rest of the sentence had been cut off when the photograph was ripped.

Larry said, "You promised me. You promised *us*. Take my hand, Brent. No! My hand!" The old man flopped to his back, still asleep.

Seb looked back at the scrapbook. Pasted to the open page was an even older-looking photo, this one wallet-sized, depicting two young boys. Seb peered closer. It, too, was captioned. "Lawrence Vincenti and Brent Auperly, blood brothers forever, July 4, 1934."

"Rock and a hard place, rock and a hard place," Larry moaned. "Why did you tell me that? *Why?*"

Now it all made sense.

Larry was one of the two boys who'd gone in search of Llewellyn's time capsule. The other boy—the one who'd died—was his dear friend Brent. Larry had nearly frozen to death, which explained his lost toes and hatred of cold. "Capt. L.," Llewellyn himself, had given him that cryptic adage about the rock and a hard place. Yet, he'd broken another promise, to give Larry his talisman before he died. Instead, he'd placed it in the capsule. And the rest was history.

"Brent, I'm sorry. Please...come back!" The old man buried his face in his pillows.

Seb fixed the blankets, then crept from the room. He lowered the thermostat to seventy degrees, still warm enough but not smothering. The old air conditioner, no doubt hardly-used, churned to life in a racket of clanks. He checked to make sure the front door was locked, then slipped out the back door, locking it, too.

He'd underestimated Larry. He'd been handicapped, had his heart broken, and lost his best friend, all at fifteen years old. That was something they had in common. He and Larry had both lost best friends.

For a fleeting moment, Chuck crossed his mind. No doubt, at that moment, Chuck was climbing in bed, spent from another day lounging around, reading comics and eating French fries. Seb had left Chuck in his wake. Seb, Inc. had no need of dead weight. They'd had a decent enough run, anyway. They'd been best friends since second grade. That was better than most of his classmates could say. Junior high always flipped the script. None of the old rules held anymore.

The rain had relented, though still falling soft. Seb stood alone on his neighbor's back stoop. He had a right to be bitter. Chuck had uttered that vile name *Timmy*, then looked on while Seb's dad chewed Seb out. So what if he'd tried to take the blame? He damn well should have taken it. Had Chuck once offered to help Seb raise cash, in order to buy the Dreamin'? No. All he'd cared about was Llewellyn's time capsule. But this was real life, not *The Goonies*. Seb's entire world was at stake. And to think Chuck had lied about being a pilot! When had he planned on coming clean? As the Dreamin' was plummeting to earth? Seb, like Brent, had been drowning. But what had his best friend done for him?

Nothing.

That was really how it really happened. Really.

Wasn't it?

It hardly mattered. In less than a month, he'd have the Dreamin'. Then whatever he said would go.

xvi.

THE BREEZE STILL SPUN with the smells of summer, but the crumpled circular at Seb's feet read "Back to School Extravaganza"—as if that wasn't an oxymoron, as if there were any such thing. Seb released the throttle bar and bent to lift the litter. Larry's lawnmower ground to a stop. The world, for an instant, seemed frozen in time: silent, still, and full of promise, poised on the brink of destiny. Then a roar of applause from the football fields pummeled the silence into submission. Seb imagined they were cheering for *him*. Seb, Inc. had reached the end zone at last. It felt a fitting send-off.

As he'd done obsessively throughout the day, he checked inside his cargo pocket for the cash he'd brought from home. After this, his very last job, he'd have three hundred dollars. He'd rush to the bank before it closed and exchange it for a certified check, which he'd promptly mail to *R/C Modeler*. With a hefty dose of luck, he'd have the Dreamin' before Labor Day. Seventh grade would be a good year, maybe even an extravaganza.

A part of him, still, would miss the chase. In spite of all the odds, he'd won—truly, fully, genuinely won. He'd *thought* he'd won a month ago, but he'd just been duped. He could have thrown the towel in, but he was made of stronger stuff.

He'd vanquished Timmy, remounted the horse, and cut the dead wood called Chuck from his life. Kit, too, had left him high and dry, whining about being overworked before she just stopped showing up. But they were all mere broken eggs; no doubt, the first of many in life. Seb was on his way.

He removed the clippings-bag from the mower and dumped it into the garbage pail. An onyx-black Saab rounded the corner and came to a stop alongside the curb. Seb recognized the car. It was Timmy and his father.

The passenger door opened. "Go," Mr. Vaughn said, "now." Haltingly, his son emerged.

But Timmy was yesterday's news. Seb said, "Come to ask for a job?"

Timmy hesitated. His father said, "Like I told you."

"But dad—"

"You want another crack?"

Looking pained, he stepped to Seb. "You've racked up quite the Sleazy Tax. I'm, um... here to collect."

The metaphor landed with a thud. Timmy was clearly parroting words. Seb said, "Come again?"

"You snaked my clients," Timmy said, regaining some of his footing.

It wasn't worth responding to. Timmy was a deposed alpha. "Two weeks 'til eighth grade—at least, your first *try* at eighth. Lots of luck." He turned.

Timmy yanked him around. "You have something of mine."

"Yeah," Seb said, "your balls."

"Nice try. You owe me what you took."

Seb laughed. Timmy, his dad, or both were delusional. "You stole my money and wrecked my airplane."

"*Your* airplane?"

"That's right. I out-competed you, fair and square. Someone finally beat you at your own game." He patted his bulging cargo pocket.

Timmy's eyes followed where Seb's hand had gone. "You were right, dad," Timmy said. Seb instantly regretted the imprudent tell. He took a step back away from Timmy. But Timmy took a bigger step closer.

Mr. Vaughn said, "Make it quick."

It sounded ominous. Seb said, "Make *what*—?"

Timmy buried a punch in his chest: a bone-crushing, superhuman punch. *Ugh!* The pain exploded deep in his gut, as if he'd been whacked with a sledgehammer. It crackled up and down his ribs. It forced the air clear from his lungs. He couldn't breathe, or call for help. He crumpled.

Timmy took a step towards the car. His father said, "Finish." Timmy wavered. His father shouted, "Now!"

Timmy reached into Seb's cargo pocket and removed the wad of cash. He stuffed it into his own pocket, then leapt inside the car. "There's a lesson in capitalism for you," Timmy's father called aloud. "*Never* be fair and square." The Saab peeled from the curb and vanished around the corner.

Seb writhed. The pain was unspeakable, and no one had seen. The doctor for whom he'd been working was out. Not even the neighborhood kids were around; no doubt, off enjoying their last days of summer—a chance that Seb had roundly squandered and, now, would never get back.

He struggled to his knees, then up to his feet. The pain began to dissipate. He drew a few sharp, choppy breaths and dusted himself off.

Life, that fickle miscreant, had shifted in a twinkling. Seb, Inc. was dead. His money was gone. Summer was all but up. He'd thought he'd hit rock bottom before, but, now, the truth was ruthlessly clear.

Rock bottom had a basement. He was moldering inside of it. But the Dreamin'—

No. The dream was dead. Full stop.

He tried to will himself to cry, but tears don't flow from broken eyes.

xvii.

THE DIN of children shouting, then splashing, roused Seb from his stupor. Adult swim, he guessed, had come to an end. In its momentary peacefulness, he'd given in to dozing. The Golden Guide spread over his eyes had barely shielded out the sun. *Birds of North America.* He flung it from his face. He knew all he needed to know about birds.

Seb tore the flap from another Fun Dip and plunged the dipstick into the powder. If he and his plans for the Dreamin' were done-for, at least he'd go out in a blaze of glory: cloying, sugar-coma glory. He had no shame, and not a fuck left to give. His family had been torn apart: mother working all hours, father despondent, sister hardly ever home. His best friend had betrayed him. Every attempt to earn a buck had ended in ignominious failure. He should've been in Ocean City, looping his newly-christened stunt plane between the coastal lookout towers, father looking on in awe. Instead, he was sprawled on an old *Garfield* towel, guzzling and sucking a slobbery swath through what remained of his accounts collectible. In less than a month, he'd be back in school. At least, then, there'd be work to distract him.

He dumped the Fun Dip into his mouth, savoring the

saccharine rush, then threw the wrapper on his ever-growing pile: soda cans and French fry troughs and sticky cherry ice cups. He buried his nose in a new Golden Guide. "Deciduous trees east of the Rockies," he said, "hmm..." Labor Day couldn't come fast enough.

"Self-pity city?" a girl's voice said. Seb raised his head.

It was Lauren.

"Don't let me interrupt your wallow," she said. She was wearing her usual soccer getup: black Sambas, Umbros, and blue and white striped Maradona jersey.

Seb's heart pulsed, then stopped just as quickly. Even Lauren in all her tomboyish glory couldn't break his funk. "What makes you think that's what I'm..." In his reflection in her sunglasses, he could see his lips were stained blood-red from cherry ice. "Oh."

She giggled that peculiar lilt only she seemed capable of. "You still owe me a hovercraft ride."

He brushed the sugar off his chest. "I owe lots of people lots of things."

"Aww," she said, "poor you. So how about it? I bet I could teach you a thing or two. Unlike you, I've actually driven a hovercraft."

Seb said, "Yeah, right."

"No, really," she said, "last summer, in France. Calais to Dover. The same route Louis Blériot flew across—"

"Across the English Channel," Seb said. He straightened up. "How do you know that?"

"Well," she said, "there's this thing called an *encyclopedia.* If there's something you want to learn about, there's a pretty good chance you'll find it in there."

"I'll have to check that out," he said. "After my wallow's finished, of course." He'd forgotten how witty Lauren could be. She'd been off-limits to him since March. Or had she? "So you rode in a hovercraft?"

"Correction," she answered, "I *drove* it. Well, at least for a few minutes. The pilot let me take the stick. We didn't crash, if that's what you're wondering."

"How come you never mentioned it?"

"You learn more by listening than by talking."

So simple, yet profound. Maybe there was something to what his mom said, that girls mature faster than boys. "Well, sorry to disappoint you. The hovercraft never got built. My dad..." He swallowed his words. He'd never shared that story with anyone. "My dad..."

"Your dad isn't you," she said.

"That's for sure."

She sat down beside him. "Penny for your thoughts, Seb?"

Playing coy was pointless now. "Just how long do you have?"

"Do your worst."

Seb said, "Don't say I didn't warn you." Then the story of summer 1989, brutal in its first telling, poured from his lips like Shakespearian tragedy. From his father's crushing blow—*You don't have what it takes*—and the clamp that crunched his father's Dreamin', to his six weeks' hard labor on Timmy's chain-gang and the abject fiasco that had been Seb, Inc., from the day-by-day collapse of his family to the violent demise of his friendship with Chuck, from the high-soaring hopes of R/C stardom to two separate piles of shattered balsa, he held back not a single thing and laid bare every gory detail. "You're up to speed," he said. "Cue the pity party."

She said, "I still want to see it."

"What?"

"Silly goose, the hovercraft."

"Where've you been?" he said, "I just told you, it *isn't*."

"I won't take no for an answer," she said. "Mopey time's over. Let's see what you've got."

*   *   *   *   *

Seb led Lauren down the stairs, careful to keep the Bilco doors quiet. The oppressive heat of the late-August sun dissipated into dank, earthen coolness. He'd long-yearned for a chance to show off for her. This wasn't how he'd expected it. "My dad doesn't like me coming down here. Too many things to break."

"Like your arm?"

"More like his equipment." Seb flicked on the lights. Some of his father's more valuable tools were missing, perhaps gone the way of his mother's lladros. From the fallout of February 17, there was no reprieve. "He could care less about my arms."

Lauren said, "I doubt that."

Had Seb actually gotten the Dreamin', his old man would have given a rip. But that dream had been ridden hard and put away wet. "Let's just say I'm fresh out of bridges to burn."

"Ah, parents," Lauren said. "But you know, Seb..." Her voice shifted from sassy to serious. "They're just making it up as they go, like you and me. The trick is knowing when they're right and when it's *you* who's right."

Seb had known Lauren since kindergarten. He'd sung "Rainbow Connection" on the stage next to her at the third-grade talent show, exchanged confetti-filled favors at Christmastime, cried when she'd cried when the *Challenger* blew. When had she become so deep? It was uncanny.

"Well, anyway..." He pulled the tarp covering his father's scrap pile, revealing a jumble of miscellany. "The *Boy's Living* hovercraft. Two by fours for the frame, PVC pipes for the air flow."

She glanced the parts over. "There's enough here for two."

"Yeah," Seb said, "and it wasn't just that. My dad and I had tweaked the plans." He pointed to the lawnmower engines.

Lauren's eyes lit up. "Cordless."

"Gasoline-powered, rear-propulsion, and steering. Basically hovering go-karts." He smiled. In that other dimension, where sometimes he strayed, Seb and his father were piloting hovercrafts, high-fiving each other with every trick turned. "Man, it would've been fun."

"It still can be," Lauren said. "Sebastian, you're a genius."

He hated the pressure that came with that word. "Huh?"

"Actually, *I'm* a genius," she said, grabbing his arm, "but I'm happy enough to play Roy to your Walt. Come with me. Your world's about to be rocked."

*   *   *   *   *

Like a prairie of asphalt and weeds, the old industrial park spread before them, punctuated, here and there, with the empty husks of factories and recreational aircraft. Piper, Cessna, Beechcraft, and more—all of them had once held stakes in a manufacturing empire. But Pennsylvania coal and steel went belly-up, and they'd left for greener pastures. In simpler times, Seb would come here and turn skateboard tricks, or jump into pickup street hockey games. But he hadn't been back since early July, when Aloysius and Rob had chased him. He said, "So why am I a genius?"

"Hovercraft races!" Lauren said. "Can't you see it?"

Seb scoffed. She'd dragged him all this way for that? The thought was ludicrous. "I can, and it's illegal. Not to mention there're no hovercrafts."

"We can fix that, and just in time, too."

"Just in time we can't be tried as adults?"

"Mind-meld with me a minute, Seb. This weekend's the town Jubilee, right?" He shrugged. She asked again, "Right?"

"I guess." He'd been indifferent to all things Jubilee.

"Well," she said, "how many times can you ride the same Ferris wheel, or go down the same super-slide on a blanket?

He let it percolate. Lauren had a point—sort of. "Well…"

"Exactly," she said. "It'd be like nothing anyone's ever seen, even better than Action Park."

That was a tall order. "Let's not get carried away, Evel Knievel. You'd need permission. The town would want to know it's safe."

"Didn't you cut Mr. Osur's lawn? He's on the town board. I'll bet he'd go to bat."

"Fat chance of that. He hates my guts."

"That old man doesn't hate anything, he just wants to see some manners. Imagine the press the town would get."

It wasn't altogether daft. But the logistics were still staggering. "Even if that actually happened—and I'm not saying it would—what about—?"

"We'll get bales of hay on loan from Harold's Farm. My sister used to work there. It's free advertising for them anyway. That's all we'd need to set up a race course here, among the factories. All that's left is to build the hovercrafts."

"Oh, is that all?" Seb said. "Other than *that*, Mrs. Lincoln, what'd you think of the play?"

"I think we're sitting on winning tickets, Seb. You want that model airplane? Time to throw a Hail Mary downfield."

Though it'd only been a couple of days, he'd banished all thoughts of having the Dreamin'. Timmy stealing his money, and the implicit threat not to resume Seb, Inc., had crushed any chance of making three hundred dollars by August 31st. He'd been able to collect cash from a few unpaid accounts, most of which he'd already spent on junk food at the pool. What Lauren was proposing was ambitious in the extreme, but maybe, just maybe, not impossible. In a perfect world, if all went right, he could make three hundred dollars—or more. But there was still one detail he'd never, ever deliver on. "Forget it," Seb said, "It's not going to happen. My dad wouldn't help, not in one million years. And even if he wanted to, he can't use his hand. His tools are verboten. The plan's dead on arrival."

Lauren said, "But he already cut some pieces, right? Three triangles for the frame and pods with beveled edges?"

"Yeah," Seb said, "So what?"

"So all that's left is the engine mount, the two by fours, and the PVC pipes."

"Don't forget the vinyl skirts," Seb said. "And how do you know so much about hovercrafts?"

"Well," Lauren said, "because Barbie has one, complete with rainbow streamers, so she and Ken can float to the prom. Imagine how green with envy Skipper will be."

Seb said, "Really?

"No, dumbass. You think you're the only one who reads *Boy's Living?* My uncle has a woodshop, too. I can get whatever tools we'd need. We can actually do this, Seb."

The plan was so aggressively nuts it could only succeed with flying colors—or crash in a blaze of ignominy. Either way, it would be epic. Lauren was a genius indeed, or certifiable. But Seb had to hand it to her. He'd have never had the balls to hope this big alone. "I *do* have some cash to make a start," he said. "The rest we'll have to buy on credit, then charge enough to make it back. Once that's done, it's all profit. Thirty races, five bucks apiece—"

"*Ahem,*" Lauren said, "correction. That's *sixty* races at five bucks apiece. Next summer the World Cup's in Italy, and hopefully so am I."

Her moxie was infectious. Maybe there was some life in the Dream. It hadn't fully eluded him yet. "All right, five bucks each, sixty races—"

"Make that *ninety,*" came a voice. They turned.

It was Chuck.

He looked out over the industrial park. "Wow, is this ever gonna be something," he said.

Seb could feel his eyes moisten. Chuck was the very last

person on earth he'd expected to see here, after all that had happened. He remembered the story old Cornball had read them: Damon and Pythias, the greatest of friends. He'd dismissed it as bunk. But he hadn't known the half of it. "Chuck," Seb said, "I don't deserve this."

Chuck shrugged. "Eh, I was in the neighborhood." He reached out his hand. Seb took it. Larry and Brent had never gotten this chance. Seb sure as hell wouldn't squander it.

Lauren placed her hand atop theirs. "This'll be one for the ages."

Seb could feel his soul take flame. The Dreamin' was still within reach.

"When do we start?" Chuck said. "Oh, and what are we doing?"

xviii.

SEB STOPPED RUNNING, doubling-over to catch his breath. Behind him, panting, straggled Chuck. A stone's-throw away, obscured by apple boughs, the gingerbread trim of the old soldier's house peeked from the trees like a sugar-spun cottage. But this was no fairy tale, and Seb no knight-errant. In a matter of minutes, he'd be a beggar. It was strangely reminiscent of his hundred-yard trudge to Larry's house last month; facing judgment, once again, at the hand of a codger with no reason to show mercy. This time it would be old Mr. Osur, terror of the Wehrmacht and linchpin of whatever hopes of glory Seb still nursed.

Chuck caught up. "I still think we should've done this first."

"Better we have something to show," Seb said. "Harder to refuse." That, and he'd been stalling.

They climbed the steps to the wraparound porch. "Or he'll get mad we jumped the gun," Chuck said.

"What did Cornball say about Alexander? Fortune favors the *what?*"

"Bold would be bypassing the town board entirely."

Chuck was Seb's own private Greek chorus, calling bullshit whenever he saw it. But friendship was more than just flattery. And Chuck, like acne, wasn't going away. "Just stick to the plan," Seb said. "It's a good one."

It had better be. From the instant they'd gone all-in on each other and the crazy idea of hovercraft races, time had buzzed at breakneck speed, only to grind to an ear-splitting halt in this, the moment that would make or break them. Seb's hands were bloody and cracked, having worked like dogs for two days straight: unloading the hovercraft parts from his basement, hauling them across town in his wagon, then doing the same for Lauren's tools, until all had been staged in the old Piper hangar they'd commandeered for a workshop. They'd begged, pleaded, wheedled, and cajoled until Uncle Enza's had agreed to sell them vinyl for skirts on credit, on top of a few other odds and ends to lend the vehicles panache. Lauren's Aunt Sue had donated her time to make the skirts with her sewing machine, in return for a free race versus her husband, with bragging rights at stake. Lauren had taken the lead on the wood, while Seb had rigged the engine and airflow, and Chuck had canvassed the town with flyers. Their work wasn't done, not by damn sight, even as their moment of truth had arrived. This next step was necessary but hardly sufficient. Around the corner at the park, the completed first of two hovercrafts sat; helmed by Lauren herself, waiting either to thank Mr. Osur or try desperately to dazzle him into changing his mind. Seb hoped to his bones it'd be the former, but he'd steeled himself for the latter.

He gulped in a stone-dry throat. "Here goes nothing." He clacked the brass door-knocker. The telltale sound of footsteps approaching sent a shiver down his spine. But what did he have to be nervous about? He was playing with the house's money.

The door creaked open. The old man peered out. Seb said, "Mr. Osur—"

"Not interested." He went to push the door closed.

Seb caught it. "I come to you with the deal of a lifetime."

"I already hired a new lawn service. I had to tell Timmy to go climb a tree. I'll thank you to do the same."

"We're not in that biz anymore," Chuck said.

"That's probably for the best. So long—"

"We're in the hovercraft business," Seb said.

Osur said, "The what?"

"Go-kart hovercrafts," Seb replied. "Scratch-built, American-made. One's all done, the second's being built." He leaned closer. "Let me cut to the chase, Mr. Osur. We want to hold races at the town Jubilee, with the industrial park for a venue. Everything is all planned out."

"And one-hundred percent safe," Chuck chimed.

They hoped. Seb nodded enthusiastically. "All we need now's the town's permission."

Osur stared incredulously. "I'd lay off the airplane glue. Nothing you said made a lick of sense. And even if I wanted to help, last I remember..." He pointed at Chuck. "You tried to stiff him in front of me, then got in my face when I called you out for it." He drew back from the door. "Lots of luck, space cadets."

"Wait." Seb grabbed the door again. Time for Plan B. He dug through his pocket for the twenty-dollar bill he'd staged there. "I shouldn't have tried to short him, you're right. You shouldn't have had to make up for it." He held out the bill. "Please accept my regrets."

Osur's stare curled into a scowl. "Does it look like I need money, son? Save your apologies for your friend."

"He already has," Chuck said, "many times." He threw his arm over Seb's shoulders. "Haven't you, buddy? We're good now, right?"

Seb said, "Absolutely. I saw the error of my ways. I said I'm sorry, over and over. I realize now I'd been greedy, but that the most important things in life you can't buy."

"I couldn't give a fig," Osur said.

"Then at least think of the town," Chuck said, initiating Plan C, as Seb had briefed him previously. "Think of the interest these races will draw—TV, newspapers...maybe even CNN!"

Osur looked puzzled. "See a *what?*"

"Never mind," Seb said. "Cable news is a joke. But otherwise Chuck's right. This'll put Stony Glen on the map. Please, just try and picture it. The lights, the crowds, the money—"

"The lawsuits. The last thing we need's a hurt or dead kid, God forbid. Last time it happened was fifty years back. Tore the whole town apart. Anyway, we've done just fine in the past without, er...whatchamacallits. Hovercars?"

"Hover*crafts,*" Seb said.

"Close enough." Again, the old man backed from the door.

"Wait!" Chuck cried. "What's that I hear?"

The grinding growl of a five-horsepower engine broke the calm of the afternoon sky. Seb sighed. Plan D was right on time.

Hovercraft One, helmed by Lauren, roared past the street corner onto the driveway. Its hull was particle board, cut in a triangle, and each of its vertexes sprouted round hover-pods with clear nylon skirts. Set center-mass was a lawnmower engine, surrounded by old car upholstery molded into the simplest of saddles, and a foam-wrapped dowel for a control stick. Ugly, crude, and resembling a prop from a 1950's sci-fi "B" movie, it motored around old Osur's yard until it reached his wraparound porch. Seb and Chuck watched admiringly as Lauren, on a cushion of air, wended her way among the trees, not harming so much as one blade of grass. The old man pressed his palms to his ears, shouting, "Turn it off!"

Lauren removed the key. Loud as a Trans Am and twice as gaudy, it settled groundward and fell silent. "Thirty miles per hour," she said. "Maybe forty on the flats. Turns like a boss and stops on a dime." She pulled off her goggles. "Just how awesome is this going to be?"

Osur sneered. "I hope you bought earplugs for the whole town."

She grinned. "Is that a yes?"

"It's impressive," he said, "but the answer's still no. The Jubilee's only two days away. How could we ever look into this?"

"What's to look into?" Seb said. "It's all right here. The course is being groomed as we speak."

"Before you got permission?" he snapped.

Chuck poked Seb in the ribs. "What'd I say?"

Seb found his most obsequious voice. In the old man's eyes, he could see he'd weakened, impressed as he was by the fruits of their labor. "Mr. Osur, *please,*" he begged, pulling the ripcord on Plan E, the last one in their repertoire, "I know where I went wrong, honest."

"He really does," Chuck said, "Believe me."

"I'd only been out for myself," Seb said. "I treated my sister and best friend like crap, but I paid for it dearly. I lost all my cash, not to mention my pride and everyone I cared about. I was a pathetic mess."

"*Was?*" Lauren said.

"Fine," Seb said, "Still am. But I'm not that jerk who spoke back to you. And even then, don't do it for *me.* My friends need this as much as I do, maybe even more. Do it for Lauren so she can see the World Cup. Do it for Chuck so he can, er... What do you need the money for?"

Chuck hemmed, "Well—"

"For the sign-up fee for Pop Warner," Lauren said. "He can kick field goals from forty-five yards, and that's in seventh grade. Someday he'll be splitting uprights for the Giants, and you can say you made it all happen."

"Yeah," Chuck said, "something like that."

Osur sighed. "That's all well and good, kids, but it changes nothing." The look on his face said he wanted to help, but not quite enough to actually do anything. "Red tape galore. Maybe next year."

Seb hung his head: he'd tried his best. Maybe it just wasn't in the cards. Osur was an immovable rock. And Dreamin' or not, he'd built a hovercraft. That, at least, was worth something. Choking up, he muttered, "Okay—"

"Hold on," Lauren said, and pushed him aside. "Mr. Osur, look. Chances like this don't grow on trees. How many times do you get to say your town held hovercraft races? Don't do it because we asked. Do it for dear Stony Glen. Do it for our civic pride. Do it for—well what do you know!" She stared past the old man, into his house, conspicuously wide-eyed and gaping. On the opposite wall, in an ornate frame, hung a poster for some old movie called *Cain and Mabel*. Seb would never have noticed it.

"That was my grandma's favorite," she said. "She had the same poster in her house, Lord rest her blessed soul. And—I know this is crazy—but Seb, Chuck, and I were just talking about naming the hovercrafts Cain and Mabel in her honor." She elbowed Seb. "Right?"

He snapped to attention. "Yup."

She said, "Right, Chuck?"

"Indeed," he said, "like I name my footballs."

She said, "Funny, but this *has* to be fate. Cain and Mabel off to the races. They'll be the glory of Stony Glen."

The old man turned around in the doorway, staring at but past the poster, seemingly into space or perhaps to vistas fondly missed. His weathered cheek twitched. His slender lips quivered. The glisten of tears welled in his eyes. "My first date with my wife we saw that picture," he said. "Sicily and Market Garden, but I never knew fear until that night. It took me three weeks to work up the nerve, so terrified I was that she'd say no. What I wouldn't give to be your age again and knowing what life had in store for me."

He cleared his throat. "We become the things we love, I guess. My dear wife would've liked you kids.

"You changed my mind, young lady," he said, "And I'm happy that you did. I suppose I'll put in a word with the town. Make sure I don't regret this. And yeah, I'd name them Cain and Mabel—that is, if you know what's good for you." He smiled and shook their hands in turn, then disappeared back into the house.

Chuck turned, brow crinkled, and said, "For real?"

Seb marveled, still not believing. "How the hell did you pull that off?"

"I already told you," Lauren said. "You learn more by listening than by talking. Pay attention to life, my friend." She pulled the goggles onto her face and climbed aboard the hovercraft. "Pick up some caffeine," she said. "Forty-eight hours goes by in a flash." She turned the key in the ignition. The tacky hovercraft roared to life, then breezed down the driveway and around the bend. "Onwards, Mabel!" Lauren bellowed.

"A veritable force of nature," Chuck said.

Seb nodded. They'd built it well. He said, "The *Boy's Living* hovercraft."

"I wasn't talking about the hovercraft," Chuck said.

They stepped off down the pebbly driveway.

xvix.

EXHAUSTED, SCRAPED, but still sanguine, Seb, Chuck, and Lauren toasted themselves with Mountain Dew, then took one final look around. Cain and Mabel, the hovercrafts, were tested, tuned, and now locked away. The course, a giant labyrinth of zigzags, flats, and hairpin turns, was ready to receive them. Mr. Osur had been good to his word: not only had the town granted permission, they'd assigned volunteers to assist. Gasoline jugs had been emplaced, course observers prepared and briefed, and paramedics notified. Water barrels were staged about, lest anyone succumb to heat. Nothing had been left to chance. A mere thirteen or so hours hence, the Piper hanger would be the hub of what, with sweat and lots of luck, would be the Jubilee's premier attraction. How, in three days, it all shook out, Seb had given it his best.

Lauren bundled her chestnut mane into a messy bun. "I still can't believe Mr. Osur said yes."

Seb said, "You suggested I ask."

"To force you to grow a pair. I didn't expect it'd actually happen."

Seb smiled in surrender. Like a boardwalk confectionary, Lauren was ever full of surprises.

Chuck said, "Lord, I hope this works."

"The odds aren't good," Lauren said. "According to the Bureau of Labor, eight of ten hovercraft businesses go belly-up in their first three days."

Chuck chomped his thumb. Seb laughed to himself. Chuck still hadn't quite gotten Lauren's sense of humor. "Quittin' time," he said. "Let's go." They locked the hangar door behind and stepped into the night.

The sky was resplendent. The stars seemed diamonds dropped in pitch; the balmy August air was tinged with the crisp of autumn fast approaching. Somewhere in the underbrush, a whippoorwill was trilling. Seb inhaled to the pit of his lungs. Soon it would be Labor Day, then seventh grade and expectations: time for football, cider, and leaves, and daily reminders he wasn't cool. Whether or not the Dreamin' would fix that, he couldn't divert from the path he'd chosen. He'd come too far to turn aside.

They crossed the catwalk over the highway, into the cluster of old, prewar homes where the factory workers once lived. A silver halo helmed the hills, the moon limning the highland lakes. "Guys," Seb said, "check it out."

Chuck's eyes spread wide. Even Lauren had to gasp, "What is it?"

"Somewhere in there," Chuck said, "is Gypsy Pond."

"Gypsy Pond?" Lauren said, "as in—?"

"The final resting place," Seb said, "of Lloyd Llewellyn's time capsule." Since coming on board, Chuck hadn't said a word about their long-forsaken quest. This moment was long overdue. Seb looked at his best friend. "Are we doing this?"

Chuck smiled so wide that Seb would've sworn his jaw had been unhinged. He reached in his backpack and drew out three Mag-lites, then tossed one to Seb and Lauren each. "Don't leave home without it."

Lauren said, "In case the urge for adventure strikes?"

"Fortune and glory," Chuck said.

They leaned into the muddy hill, overgrown with milkweed. The going was rough, made worse by darkness: they staggered and stumbled and trundled ahead, keeping, as best they could, to the trail. Like the sun-bleached bones of an elephant graveyard, the corroded husk of the old power plant loomed ghoulishly above. The last time Seb had passed this way, Aloysius and Rob had been hard on his heels, and he afraid of Indian-burns or, at worst, a wedgie. But that had been another world. It seemed forever and a day ago.

Lauren, losing her balance, spilled into Seb's arms. He caught her, gently, by the waist and helped her to her feet. The warmth of her body against his felt sweet. "Thanks," she said. "The payoff had better be worth all this."

Chuck said, "Not feeling the love?"

"Nope," she replied, "just bug bites and burrs."

"Imagine, if you will," he said, "these are not the woods outside Stony Glen, but the dark, forbidding Argonne forest of northeastern France. The date is October 6, 1918. The Germans, freed from the Eastern Front now that Russia has surrendered, have risked everything on a final, all-out assault. Only an Allied counterattack, spearheaded by the American army, can save the war from being lost. You are Private Dickie White, mint-green and fresh from basic training. Your unit, the One Hundred and Twenty-Eighth, has been charged with taking, then holding, a bald, exposed hilltop called by the generals *L'endroit mourant.*"

Lauren said, "The dying place?"

"Correct," Chuck said. "No one's been able to keep it for long. Push the German army off, their airplanes simply strafe the ridge, then their soldiers take it back.

"But back to Private White. You and your rifle company have managed to dislodge the Germans but only at horrendous cost. The bodies of your buddies from home, plus those of the Brits and French in support, are piling in bloody heaps beside you. The units you were told were coming to help are nowhere to be found. You can hear the Germans in the woods all around, biding their time for a counter-attack. You're ordered to form a defensive perimeter, but you know it'll do no good. You're almost out of ammunition. You're almost out of time. You're out of all but the faintest of hope. And that's when you hear it."

"Hear what?" Seb said.

"The glorious, thundering, high-pitched whine of the Spad VII biplanes of the One Hundred Third Aero Squadron. Like a Valkyrie, or Angel of Death, one of them swoops from the gunwale-gray sky and strafes the woods in front of you. Back and forth, at least twelve times, it dives so low its wheels brush the treetops, firing into the dark wood line, coolly indifferent to the hail of lead spit forth from German machine guns. Back and forth, back and forth...it strafes the wood, then banks about and strafes the wood again and again. German bodies, like sandbags, pile high. German airplanes challenge him, but he shoots down every one of them. Your company bravely holds the hill until the battalion sent to relieve you appears. One final time he strafes the wood, then dips a wing low in gallant salute and speeds away to rejoin his squadron. You march to the rear, lucky to have lived—and live you will, to your ninety-first year. You write in your diary about what you'd seen: the magnificent lord of the sky who'd saved you, and risked so much to win the day. And it's a fortunate thing you did, lest it be lost forever, for the pilot would never speak aloud of it, eschewing as he did fame and glory.

"That pilot, as I'm sure you can guess, was the man whose time capsule we're about to find. So, yes—what we're doing is all worth it."

Lauren rolled her eyes. Seb could only gasp. He'd never appreciated Chuck's gift of gab until now.

They crested the crown of the treacherous ridge. Before

them, like a silver plain, lay a watery expanse. Chuck said, "There it is."

Gypsy Pond.

It was enormous, more like a lake; it spread, with speed, to each horizon. Along its edge, every hundred yards, the pond branched off into a stream, each of them snaking back into the woods. Some ten feet from where they stood, the land ran flat along the pond, dotted with scrub and little trees: all that remained, no doubt, of what had been a bathers' beach. Past it lay a fat boulder and just beyond that, a cement slab, likely once a gazebo's base.

Seb sighed. Though the water shimmered bright as foil, they could barely see to the other side. They could search all summer and not find themselves closer to what they were looking for.

Lauren said, "Could we narrow it down to maybe an acre? A square mile at the least?"

"Forget it," Chuck said, "this would take half a year. We'll come back after the Jubilee, get some others to help us."

Seb could feel Chuck's disappointment. Had he been less self-absorbed all summer, they might have started searching in June. As it stood, if they started searching now, even optimistically, they'd have to break in mid-November and resume, at best, late March. By then, anything could happen. And there was no guarantee of success.

"I'm sorry," Seb said, meaning it.

"Eh," Chuck said, "bad timing. Tomorrow's what's important."

Like Damon and Pythias, friends like Chuck didn't grow on trees. Seb turned to walk back down the hill. And then, quite apropos of nothing, a memory danced across his mind.

Larry.

"Wait," Seb said. "Hold on." They stopped.

"Larry," Seb whispered, "Larry, Larry." Why hadn't he thought of this before? "What was it Larry told me?"

Chuck said, "Huh?"

So much had occurred since their falling-out. Seb had forgotten to fill Chuck in. *"Between a rock and a hard place,"* Seb said, *"then as far as your feet will carry you. That's where you'll find what really matters."*

Lauren looked askance. "Good one, Mr. Miyagi."

"It's what Llewellyn told Larry," Seb said. "He'd promised him his talisman. But he hid it here, instead."

Seb looked closer at the beach. Between the boulder on one side, and the ruined gazebo's base on the other, a small, almost imperceptible, rivulet ran, snaking downhill into the dark. *"Between a rock and a hard place...* Of course!"

The revelation burst to light. Llewellyn *had* given Larry the key, only Larry had never realized. For fifty years he'd carried the adage, treating it as life advice, never knowing its real meaning. "Between a rock and a hard place," Seb said. "The boulder and the slab. We follow that creek. Where it ends we'll find the time capsule."

"A coded clue," Lauren said. "How droll."

Chuck closed his eyes and whispered solemnly, "It all makes perfect sense. He had to reveal *without* revealing, to proclaim from the housetop what he'd kept in whispers, to—"

"To screw with that guy Larry's head," Lauren said, "and countless other fanboys like you. A map would've been so much easier." She stepped off along the beach. "No time like the present," she said. "Are you coming?"

The shaggy woods engulfed them anew. The stream, a meandering trail of light, sliced a ravine through the gathering gloom. They stumbled downhill along its bank, slipping hither and tither on stones and batting saplings from their eyes. Time seemed to stand still, the further they pushed. Up ahead, the shimmering stopped and gave way to pitch-darkness. Seb, in the moonlight, looked at his watch. They'd been walking for half an hour. "As far as your feet will carry you," he said.

The tiny stream threw one last loop, cascading down a heap of rocks, expiring in a limpid pool. Though overgrown with ferns and moss, with water flowing over them, that the rocks had been purposely placed was clear. They formed a simple, elegant shrine. The capsule had to be inside.

"Just like *Romancing the Stone*," Lauren said.

Chuck looked at Seb. "You doing the honors?"

Even before Seb longed for the Dreamin', he'd yearned for this very moment, when Llewellyn's time capsule lay at his feet. But Chuck had yearned for it even more. Seb handed him a thick oak branch. "Llewellyn would have preferred you."

Chuck pushed it away. "You cracked the code."

Damon and Pythias, indeed. "I got lucky," Seb said. "You kept the dream alive."

Chuck hesitated. "But you—"

"Sorry to ruin your love-fest, boys," Lauren said, grabbing the branch, "but tomorrow's kind of a busy day, in case you've forgotten." She slapped it into Chuck's hand. "Clearly, your life has built to this."

"I like you more and more," Chuck said. He raised the branch above his head. "Stand aside."

Seb took Lauren by the hand and led her a safe distance. Chuck speared the branch against the shrine. It landed with a hollow thud. Mud splattered but the rocks held fast. "Try winching underneath," Seb said.

Chuck wiggled the branch into the base, then pulled hard, up against it. The shrine groaned but kept together. "Hmm..." he said, then rolled a cylindrical rock underneath, as a fulcrum. "Come give me a hand."

Careful not to snap the branch, the three of them pushed down. The shrine quavered, rattling softly. "We're close," Chuck said. "I felt it. Again!" Seb dug his knees into the ground. He arched his back, rolled his shoulders, and heaved against the lever-branch.

Crack!

The top stones burst, the shrine crumbled. A cavalcade of salamanders and water beetles scurried out. The waterfall spilled down the bank, carrying off the slimy mud and washing clean the old shrine-stones. The three of them shined their Mag-lites closer. Although obscured by moss and twigs, a faint metallic sheen shined back. Seb pointed to it. "There."

Chuck plunged his hands into the muck and gently drew them out again. Between his palms was a metal urn.

Lloyd Llewellyn's time capsule.

Seb bowed his head. Chuck held it aloft, like Excalibur, then asked Lauren, "Impressed yet?"

"Let's not get carried away, Geraldo. How 'bout you open it first?"

He set it on the ground beside them. Seb ran his hand along its edge and rinsed it off in the flowing water. It was, as best he could tell, a vintage tin coffee can. Whatever paint that once adorned it was gone, but in spite of fifty years in the mud, it was startlingly well-preserved. A lid was fastened to the top, secured by three corroded screws. Chuck pulled out his Swiss Army Knife and selected the Phillips-head screwdriver.

Lauren said, "Fat chance, Bob Vila. Those screws are rusted tight. Allow me." She took the can and knife from Chuck, then flipped up the serrated blade.

"Careful," Chuck said. "We don't know what's inside."

"I'm betting it's not a mummy," she said. She clutched the can between her knees and gently sawed a hole in the top. It clunked to the bottom of the can.

Chuck gasped, "It's empty?"

Lauren held her Mag-lite up, then peered an eye inside. Seb said, "What do you see?"

"Wonderful things," she said. "Have a look." She handed it to Seb.

He took it, like relics, into his hands. Chuck held the light steady, watching over Seb's shoulder. Seb reached his fingers inside the can. They brushed against what felt like leather. He pinched it through the hole in the lid. The light revealed a drawstring purse. "Open it," Chuck said.

Seb undid the drawstring and tilted the purse. Waiting to feel the cold of jewels, instead there was only the slightest of wisps of paper in his palm. He held it to his eyes. "What the...?"

It was a faded scrap of photograph paper, a few inches across and torn on one side, not unlike any piece of debris one might find in the gutter.

"There's writing on the back," Chuck said.

Seb flipped it around. Sure enough, in rough cursive, an inscription had been scrawled. He peered closely and read aloud, "Is right beside you."

Chuck raised an eyebrow. "Huh?"

Seb's blood ran cold. He knew exactly what it was. Not one week ago, he'd seen its other half. "My God," he whispered, "of course."

It was the missing piece of the photograph from Ashy Larry's scrapbook, the one on which Llewellyn had promised Larry his treasures when he'd reached Valhalla. The symmetry of life was sublime—and uncanny. "*What really matters*," Seb said, "*is right beside you.*"

"Well," Lauren snarked, standing, "is that ever one to grow on." She waved her hand dismissively.

But it was.

Seb's mind sped back to one month ago, right before Timmy crashed the Dreamin'. Chuck had asked him if he thought Llewellyn might wonder about his friends. He'd gruffly dismissed the inquiry: Llewellyn neither had nor needed friends, and all he'd done, he'd done alone. But he'd been so very wrong. *What really matters is right beside you.* Those words rang truer than he'd ever know.

Nothing Llewellyn had done was alone. Before he could strafe that perilous ridge, someone had had to prepare his airplane; someone had had to load up his guns. Someone had had to build that biplane. Someone had had to teach him to fly. Someone from the depths of his past had to show him how to be a man, and instill his love of country. Someone had ever been there, beside him. Seb said, "It's so true."

Seb looked to his left and then to his right, flanked as he was by Lauren and Chuck. If not for them, where would he be? Certainly, not here—and nowhere near the edge of glory, so tantalizingly close to achieving his goal of piloting the Dreamin'. That hope would have died a long time ago. Instead, together, they'd wrought from scratch a final, once-in-a-lifetime chance. What really mattered *was* right beside him. What really mattered was them.

Seb put his arms over his friends' shoulders. "Boy, am I one lucky dude."

"You're not cool enough for dude status yet, Seb," Chuck said. "But maybe soon."

"I'll take that as a compliment." He slipped the photo scrap back in the bag, then stuffed it in his pocket. "Thanks."

"Don't thank us yet," Lauren said. "This weekend's going to tell the tale. Check your ego at the door."

They staggered up the draw to the beach, then turned and walked back down the hill. "I can't help but feel let down," Chuck said.

"Eh," Lauren said, "life happens."

"Yeah, but it was just some old junk. It was supposed to be the key to Llewellyn's glory as a pilot."

Seb said, "But it was."

Chuck said, "How do you figure?"

"Please, no," Lauren said. "We need to go sleep off all this excitement. Piper hangar, eight o'clock sharp."

They exchanged high-fives, then went separate ways. The evening lingered still as the grave, its serenity broken only by crickets. Seb waited until he was alone, then threw a final look at the moonlight-crowned highlands, where some fifty years ago Llewellyn had hidden his legacy and Larry and Brent had dared to seek it. Poor Brent would never come home again. But long before they'd braved the cold, he and Larry had already found the talisman that changed their lives.

They had had each other.

Seb swung his eyes towards home. The next few days would indeed tell the tale.

XX.

THE FLUSH OF MORNING rent the east and spilled like treasure across the floor. Once again in what seemed nigh forever, Seb leapt from the sheets in their Kit-less bedroom and shuffled into work clothing. He'd purposely slept with the blinds drawn back, lest he fail to rise with the sun. It was Friday morning, August 25th: Day One of Jubilee. The verdict of the next three days would echo long across his life. Many a morning had begun like this, only to end in failure and pain, widening the chasm 'twixt him and the Dreamin'. But today was different, and palpably so. He threw a glance at the *Boy's Living* issue, propped like a broadside on his bookshelf. Every road, somehow, led back to it. There was nowhere to go but onwards.

He tiptoed past his sleeping parents, catching a glimpse of his father's bad hand. In six months, it had healed well enough, though the scar would never fully fade. It looked like a shiny, slender earthworm. To think that such a little thing had set so much in motion. He downed a bowl of cereal and sidled out the door.

Dunbar Drive was sleepy yet, Ashy Larry's house still dark. He stepped off briskly towards downtown. At the corner, in the distance, the line of trees of the sanctuary loomed, veiled in morning mist. Seb, Inc. had sprung to life in their shade, only to die an inglorious death weeks later on a doctor's lawn. But that was all behind him now.

His stride picked up as he crossed Boulder Road. The spires of his school broke the haze. From here, he could look both backwards and forwards. What if he hadn't called Lauren Guinevere, or been shanghaied by Timmy? Seventh grade was bigtime: what tribulations lay in store? The Dreamin', he prayed, would soften all blows. But he still had to get it.

He passed the train station, deli, and bank, with bittersweet pangs as he stepped past the theater. Beneath the *The Abyss'* nautical decor, bits of yellow confetti peeked out, the dross of Batmania, like pottery-shards in some Bronze Age barrow. It had been a summer's glory, reduced to history's dustbin. Passing the pawnshop, he waved to Rand, unlocking the grills from its plate-glass windows. He could see six of his mother's lladros, first pawned, then sold for cut-rate cash. But that had been his mother's choice, same as Ocean City. He could only shoulder so much blame.

The fairgrounds teemed with motion and sound, the citizens of Stony Glen clinging feverishly to summer's shirttails. Even at not-quite eight o'clock, they were fast perusing the farmers' markets, trying their hands at carnival games, and bounding among the many bounce-castles. Seb recognized his classmates' parents and many he'd met landscaping with Timmy. He'd normally try to avoid them all. But there was nothing left to hide. He strode through the center of the festivities and out to the old industrial park.

Lauren and Chuck were already there, the volunteers heading off to their posts. An ambulance was parked nearby, with paramedics milling. The hovercrafts were staged at the line. By the telltale smell of gasoline, their racing legs had already been stretched and the course given a final once-over. Though the big throngs wouldn't arrive until noon, a crowd of onlookers had already gathered. Front and center was a familiar face.

"Mr. Cornwall," Seb said, "top o' the morning."

"And a halcyon morning it is," Cornball said, climbing from a lawn chair. "I've been waiting since six, want my name in the books. First annual Stony Glen hovercraft racer ever."

The thought gave him jitters. "Annual," Seb said, "as in we have to do this every year?"

"Let's just get through today," Lauren said, and threw her arms around Seb's and Chuck's shoulders. "Nervous, boys?"

"No," Chuck said.

Seb said, "A little."

"Well, buck up," she said. "It's always darkest just before pitch black." She broke from the huddle, brimming with verve, and cried, "Who wants head-to-head with Mr. Cornwall?"

A fusillade of arms went up. Lauren grabbed a fourth-grade girl who'd lost her mother to cancer this year, but had never lost her smile. "You're a perfect match for Ms. Mabel, Kelli," she said. "Tough as nails yet dainty."

Seb collected the riders' money, inhaling to the pit of his soul. They were crossing into virgin outlands: any number of things could go wrong, a fiasco worthy of cable news. But he'd come too far to come just this far. In the bowels of some distant warehouse, his Dreamin' waited on *him*. And that, in the end, was all that mattered.

He plopped a helmet on Cornball's head. "Throttle backwards, brake forwards, steer left and right like a go-kart. Follow the arrows. Mind the barriers." He yanked the engine's starter cord.

Chuck pulled Mabel's; the hovercrafts roared. Seb slapped Cornball's back. "Go get 'em!" Lauren did the same for Kelli, then ran to the starting line.

She raised aloft a checkered flag. "Three, two, one," she bellowed, "*Go!*"

The hovercrafts, like Indy cars, sped off down the straightaway, vanishing in clouds of dust and gasoline exhaust. The crowd, mesmerized, whistled and hooted. Seb scrambled atop the ten-foot ladder they'd positioned at the finish line. From his vantage, the hovercrafts looked like toys. "Come on," he said, "no snafus, no crashes...*come on...*"

"Here we go," Chuck said, "Tomba's Twist."

Decelerating off the straightaway, the hovercrafts motored into a slalom, Chuck's brainchild and favorite part of the course. "Yeah," Chuck cried, "just look at 'em go!" They wended between the flagpole gates, switching back and forth the lead, then flipped into a hairpin turn and into the cavernous Beechcraft factory.

"Moment of truth," Lauren said. If anything was going to go wrong, the factory was where.

The volunteer at the gates gave thumbs-up. Seb craned his neck for a better view. Rattling off the old brick walls and tinny window-frames, the whine of the hovercrafts' engines echoed, sounding especially fierce. The crowd collectively held its breath. Seb could see flashes of color and motion, Cain and Mabel zipping about the twists and turns inside the ruin. Then all sound and motion stopped. They'd entered the old wind tunnel shaft.

An anxious hush fell over the crowd. Chuck said, "Neither light nor sound escapes the Black Hole."

Seb nodded. They'd planned it to astonish the crowd, and it had with flying colors. Lauren glanced at her stopwatch. "Right on time," she said. "Five, four, three, two—"

Old Cornball on Cain burst out of the factory, pumping his fist high over his head and crowing like a rooster. Mere seconds behind popped Kelli on Mabel, grim-faced and determined, hands clutching the yoke. They motored down the back straightaway, Kelli creeping ever closer, feeding off the roar of the crowd, then threw themselves through another hairpin and into the treacherous Corn Maze.

Seb said, "Hope they paid attention." If they had, inside the factory, they'd have seen the key to the Corn Maze: an aerial view map, highlighting a shortcut. Otherwise, they'd poke about, wasting precious seconds.

The sound of engines throttling back gurgled from the bales of hay. "I'm guessing they didn't," Chuck said.

The maze had been Seb's idea. He'd tried to mix enjoyment with challenge, and thought he'd struck a good enough balance. But the crowd was visibly on-edge. And design flaws weren't quick fixes. He said, "Should we have—?"

The engines boomed alive again. Mabel, like a bat from hell, surged between the haystack walls, Cain hard on her coattails, and throttled go-for-broke top speed down the final straightaway. Railing, the crowd willed them on, "Go, go, go, *go!*"

Seb, Chuck, and Lauren, clenched fists and teeth, could only silently look on—part in terror, part with joy—at their creations' coming-out party. "One hundred meters," Seb said, "now fifty...twenty...ten..."

The hovercrafts buzzed across the finish line, Kelli ahead by a nose. Lauren waved the checkered flag. The crowd erupted in cheers of joy. The hovercrafts settled to the pavement. "Worth the wait tenfold!" Cornball yelled. "Reading the classics, sipping Earl Gray, just ain't gonna cut it no mo'."

His attempts to sound streetwise were mortifying. "Sorry, Mr. C.," Seb said. "Close second isn't bad."

"I know, but I'll be back," he said.

Exhilaration washed over Seb. The first race had gone off without a hitch and by their reaction the crowd wanted more. He couldn't help but feel sanguine. "Only eighty-nine more," he said, tongue-in-cheek. Between debt and expenses, they'd soon found out, they'd have to run far more than ninety. But the number just felt good to say.

"Eighty-nine in eighty-nine," Lauren said. "Poetic symmetry."

Cornball climbed from Cain. "I see the gardener's boy's come into his own," he said, "neither with sword nor armor."

He'd forgotten The Once and Future King. "Just the magic of hovercrafts," Seb said.

Cornball shook Seb's hand. "Magic, to be sure," he said.

"All right," Chuck cried, "who's next?"

The clamoring crowd lurched towards Cain and Mabel. Lauren grabbed a can of green spray paint and drew a waiting-queue and corral. "Pair up," she said, "or we'll find you a match. Grudge-holders and bragging rights-seekers welcome."

Time, that fickle dramaturge, took off at a gallop. Anxious riders paid their fares, then sped away to thrills. Seb loaded and debriefed one and all, welcoming the accolades but sharing them with Chuck and Lauren. The verdict seemed unanimous: not only was it an inspired thought, the execution had been flawless. Inside the black-lit factory, one might be forgiven for thinking he was aboard *Nostromo,* dodging alien stowaways; the Corn Maze evoked Halloween horrors; and the whipping wind in the slalom and straightaways reminded riders of snowbound sleigh-riding. Seb relished it all with a grain of salt, no stranger to apparent triumph, only to see the rug pulled beneath. But even now, he could taste his dream getting closer and closer, and he wasn't slowing down.

"Payback time," came Cornball's voice.

Seb looked up. He and Kelli were back in the corral.

"Already?" Seb said. It couldn't have been two hours. He'd been too busy to look at the line, but it had to have been longer than *that.*

"Hold up." He ran to the side of the hangar. Sure enough, to his dismay, the line—if one could call it that—barely made it to the other side. The crowd that had watched the first races had mostly dissipated. Though the fairgrounds in the distance thronged, there was little, if any, commerce between them. Even allowing for the early hour and the fact that it was a weekday, at this rate, they'd never complete enough races.

Cain and Mabel thundered off. "Where is everybody?" Seb said.

"I think I know," Mr. Schultz said. He was standing in line beside two kids, by their semblance to him, his grandchildren.

"Where?" Seb said.

Schultz held up tattered fliers. "The things you find in martin nests. I'm guessing these were all ripped down."

"By birds?"

"Not a chance." He pointed to each of the flier's edges, torn off at the staples. "This is the work of *Homo sapien,* and I'm guessing the young, delinquent kind."

The suspect list was too long to rehash, but squarely at the top perched three: Timmy, Rob, and Aloysius. Any one of them could, and would, have done it, to revel in Seb's anguish. But that was then, and this was now, and self-pity wouldn't put riders in queue.

He knelt beside Schultz's grandchildren. "I'll give you each a free ride for your help—maybe *two* if you really come through."

The kids, both about ten years old, grinned and answered, "Okay."

"I need you to go to the fairgrounds," Seb said. "Run through the crowd, shout 'til your lungs hurt. Tell everyone about the hovercraft races. Get other kids to help if you can. Get everybody here."

"You got it," they said and scampered away, vanishing across the flats and into the Jubilee crowd, then barking like medieval heralds, "Hovercraft races! Come one, come all!"

"Clever," Mr. Schultz said. "Oh, and Sebastian, by the

way, if the hovercraft business proves too taxing, there's an opening next spring at the sanctuary. I could use someone like you. You're all heart." He smiled and stepped out of line.

Seb, emotions swirling, could barely utter a heartfelt "thank you" before the stampede caught his eye. Out of the Jubilee crowd, nearly every tween and teenager in town was running uphill towards the course, yelling smack.

"You're going down!"

"What, like your mom did last night?"

"Let's see if you can crack jokes when you're choking on my dust."

"Oh, like your mom was choking on my—"

"Excuse me," Seb cried, "enough said...right this way. And we're a family-friendly establishment, mind you."

Morning broke to sunny noon. Seb, Lauren, and Chuck continued to grind: assist riders, observe the race, record times, run safety checks, then do it all over again from the top. Cain and Mabel, those noble chariots, rocketed down the circuit and back, neither slowing nor wearing down. Lauren had cobbled them skillfully, as well as Seb's father could ever have done, and Chuck had loading down to a science. But time and gasoline leached away, forcing them to take turns scrambling into town on fuel-runs. Afternoon found their profits diminishing. To raise fares now would be unseemly; tomorrow, they'd have to work harder, and faster. But confidence was running high and Stony Glen enthralled.

Or was it?

Lauren pointed. "Are you seeing this?"

Seb turned. Although the line was a robust length, the mood of the people in it was not. Some were griping or snapping at others about their places. Some were even stepping away, or storming off in frustration.

"Their loss," Chuck said.

Lauren replied, "Not really."

She was right. "Repeat business," Seb said. "If people stop coming back, we're screwed."

"And if the line's this long," Lauren said, "first-timers won't want to wait, either."

Chuck said, "How about return vouchers?"

It was as good a quick-fix as another. Seb said, "I'll get post-its—"

"Hold up," Lauren said. "That'll piss off the people who decide to wait, the sight of others skipping the line."

"Yeah, but anyone can get one," Chuck said.

"No matter," she said. "We can only load two at a time, and our turnover rate's between twelve and fifteen minutes. *That's* our problem."

Seb racked his brain. "Should we build two more?" It sounded even more absurd having escaped his lips.

Lauren laughed. "You understand the concepts of *profit* and *time,* don't you?" She grabbed the spray paint can. "Chuck, load the riders. Seb, follow me." She ran off towards the Corn Maze.

Delirious teenagers at their sticks, Cain and Mabel disappeared inside just as Seb and Lauren arrived. The riders' shrieks echoed through the bales of hays' walls. The racket warmed Seb's heart. Each voice was worth five dollars.

"We need to cut out this loop," Lauren said.

Now it was Seb's turn to laugh. "Do *you* understand the concept of *fun?* The Corn Maze is our bread and butter."

"And the slowest part of the course," she said.

"No way. Water down the fun too much, they'll just go somewhere else."

"Trust me," Lauren said, "they won't. We're still light-years cooler than the Tilt-a-Whirl, even. We'll keep getting repeat riders, and first-timers will have shorter waits. We'll take everyone's time and seed them. Sunday, we'll reopen this loop and make it a race-off."

The optics were hard to countenance, even if the logic

wasn't. But her heart was in this as much as his own. And so far, her instincts had been spot-on. "Fine—"

"Avast, ye lubbers!" Aloysius and Rob, in pirate hats and painted-on beards, leapt over the bales of hay into the course, just as the hovercrafts popped from the maze.

"Move, douchebags!" Lauren said.

They spread their legs and arms out wide. The riders throttled Cain and Mabel back, swerving to miss the live obstacles and toppling bales of hay on both sides.

Rob twirled his plastic scimitar. "That was just too close for comfort, like that show with Cosmic Cow."

"Another," Aloysius chimed, "and the town just might think twice 'bout this."

Lauren said, "And you'll both be cooling your heels downtown."

Aloysius laughed, "How's that unlike any other day?"

"Yeah," Rob said, "the five-o love us. You try making quota in this one-horse town."

The riders gathered their wits, flipped off Aloysius and Rob, and thundered down the home straightaway. But Seb wasn't letting them off quite so light. He stepped into their pimply faces. "Who tore down my fliers?"

"Summer school bites ass," Rob said.

"You should've just went with it," Aloysius said. "Some things aren't meant to be. Now everyone knows how gay you are, and when all's said and done you'll still be in the red."

It was as much a confession as he'd ever get. Seb's better angels urged forgiveness. But they'd once again set him back from his goal. And he wasn't feeling magnanimous. He grabbed the spray paint can from Lauren. "Maybe I'll be in the red, but at least I won't be green with envy."

They drew blanks. Rob grunted, "What—?"

Seb sprayed their faces full of paint. They crumpled, clutching their heads. Seb shook the paint can vigorously, and for good measure sprayed their necks, backs, and arms. The crowd, who'd been watching it all, brayed its thunderous approval. "Now hit the road," Seb said.

Aloysius and Rob, shamed, scampered off, wailing, "You haven't heard the last of us!"

Lauren stepped beside him. "Have we?"

Seb handed her back the paint can. "Who cares?" They moved the bales of hay, closing the Corn Maze, and ran back to the starting line. The crowd, predictably, was inclined to grumble, but Seb explained why, and about the Sunday race-off, and in no time, clearly, they'd accepted its wisdom.

Afternoon plodded to balmy evening. The sky darkened as the coffers greened up. Like thoroughbreds, Cain and Mabel raced on, with only minimal tune-ups needed. Old Cornball returned for several more tries, spouting poetry with each finish crossed and trying to one-up himself. Only with nightfall did the crowd dissolve. Rumors swirled that some high-schoolers had taken to keeping books on the races. Whether or not it was true, it brought a mercurial grin to Seb's face. But he wasn't out of the woods yet, not by damn sight.

He sorted, then counted the first day's earnings. "Four hundred and fifty dollars," he said. "Not bad, with our slow start and fuel runs." It was an auspicious debut but hardly a coup: really, they'd just zeroed out. Friday had been the warm-up. Saturday and Sunday would be the main event.

Chuck said, "We should buy extra gas now, store it for tomorrow."

"Good idea." Seb peeled off fifty dollars.

Lauren snatched it from his hand. "We have bigger problems than that," she said. "It's going to pour tomorrow."

xxi.

SEB'S HEART SANK. "Are you kidding?"

She tuned the radio. The earworm jingle of 1010 WINS chimed. "I overheard riders," she said. "Listen up."

The radio crackled, then a garbled voice said, "Showers in the forecast for the a.m., heavy at times, tapering off to afternoon clouds, then giving way to clear skies. Temperature well into the eighties with a nasty heat index... so ladies, mind those perms."

Chuck switched it off. "Hairnet time, Lauren."

"I'm Norman French," she said, "Part Viking. You know what a Blood Eagle is?" Chuck pretended to shudder in fear.

But inclement weather was serious business. "Focus, you two," Seb said. "All right, so we move the queue inside the hangar and periodically brush down the course."

Lauren said, "As if they were race cars."

Seb didn't follow. "Your point being?"

"Rainy course makes no difference," she said. "They float on air. There's nothing to grip. But Cain and Mabel are ash and pulp-board. They aren't meant to get soaking wet."

Chuck said, "Well, whose fault is *that?*"

"I didn't see your ass on the chop saw," she said. "They had to be light or they wouldn't, you know, *hover.* They'll be like soggy noodles."

Chuck said, "So we wait until it's dry."

"What happened to fortune favors the bold?" Seb said.

"Postpone and we might as well cancel," Lauren said. "We'll never make up that kind of shortfall. And, in case you hadn't noticed, this isn't exactly a blimp hangar, and no one'll want to stand out in the rain. Dollars to donuts the *town* shuts us down, at least for a few hours."

Seb roiled. Like the photograph in *Back to the Future,* in his mind the Dream began to fade. Permission or none, morning racing was essential; otherwise, they'd fall back in the red, just as Aloysius had taunted. There was no use sitting on playable cards with so much at stake. And thinking things through a few steps ahead had begun to come second-nature.

He swiped the fifty dollars back from Lauren, grabbed an equivalent amount from the cash box, and handed all of it to Chuck. "Get lacquer, brushes, and trash bags, Chuck. Lauren, grab pen and paper and come with me."

She said, sarcastically, "Where to, boss?"

"An unassailable position," Seb said. He knew what to do.

*   *   *   *   *

What a wonder is the hovercraft! Part airplane, part car, part sled, and part boat, it straddles each epoch of man's ingenuity: yesterday's dream, today's marvel, tomorrow's commonplace. A Victorian dream, a steampunk vision, a wartime need turned postwar reality, it does yeoman's work for its maker when asked and demands but the littlest care in return. Its soul is fun disguised as grit. How droll to ride on a biscuit of air within a world of wheels and keels. How epic to traverse the sea, land, and ice on one's own micro-atmosphere, for the hovercraft goes everywhere and pays its rider's trust back tenfold.

But even among hovercrafts, Cain and Mabel were specimens. *Boy's Living,* since the 1950's, had been hawking plans for them, built around canister vacuum engines. If properly built, they'd be wobbly and slow, and tethered to an electrical socket. Seb and his father had tweaked the design, substituting gasoline for electricity and adding thrusters on the back. If someone had thought to do this before, Seb was not aware of it. He'd been a pioneer.

He beamed as he watched his creations thunder home. Lauren called out, "Five thirty-five! The rain's hardly slowing them at all."

"From your lips to God's ears," Chuck said.

Seb checked his watch: it was 9:15 a.m. They'd been racing for over an hour, and so far, so good. The forecast, for once, had been right. It had steadily rained since sunrise, throwing a damper on the town Jubilee, but not on the spirits of the morning's racers, who'd still turned out in force. They huddled in the hangar awaiting their turn, or cheered on the others from the comfort of their complimentary trash-bag ponchos. Seb, Chuck, and Lauren had barely slept, slathering lacquer all over the hovercrafts into the wee hours. They were sturdier now, if a mite heavier. With every race, the Dream crept closer. But the real obstacle had yet to be faced. And now, that obstacle was shuffling their way.

Seb patted the laminated page in his pocket. He'd secured them an insurance policy. "Here comes Mr. Osur," he said. "Just act natural." He glanced at Chuck, who was shadow-boxing, reciting lines from *Rocky IV*. "Actually," he said, "in your case, Chuck, don't."

Chuck snapped to attention. Lauren, ready with her lines, nodded Seb's way. Osur sidled through the crowd. Seb pretended not to notice, but kept a close watch through the side of his eye. He'd rehearsed this scene in his mind several times.

The rain, momentarily, intensified. Osur cleared his throat, "Ahem."

Seb spun in fake surprise. "Oh, Mr. Osur, didn't see you sneak up. Come to admire Cain and Mabel?"

The soldier raised a cupped hand, rapidly filling with rainwater. "Didn't think you kids'd be mudding it," he said, laying his disapproval thick.

"Oh, you know," Seb said, deflecting, "neither rain nor snow nor dark of night." He pulled the laminated list from his pocket and made a show of perusing it. "Next up," he cried, "Doug and Colin."

The riders, eight-year-old boys in raincoats and galoshes, ran from the crowd, high-fiving each other and climbing aboard the hovercrafts. Chuck and Lauren loaded them up, then started their engines and waved them away. Seb said, "You see? A little rain never hurt anyone."

"This is more than a little rain," Osur said. "And you should've been at the meeting last night. I'd figured you'd gotten the message. Shut down for now and we'll play it by ear. It's not supposed to go later than noon."

"No can do," Chuck said.

The old man said, gruffly, "Excuse me—"

"Mr. Osur," Lauren said, shoving Chuck away, "we'd be happy to, really happy to, but..."

"But what?"

"Well," she said, "it's no skin off *our* back, but you just can't do that to *them*." She pointed to the waiting queue, coiled inside the Piper hangar. "We've already sold out every time slot."

The old man looked puzzled. "What?"

"That's right," Seb said. "Last night, at the exit, we set up shop, selling reservations. Each six-minute block 'til one o'clock is prepaid and spoken for."

He said, "Then un-prepay and un-speak for them."

"I wish we could," Seb said, "but try to understand. Yesterday's lines were far too long, so we came up with this idea." He held up the laminated list. "Signed, sealed, delivered. And so far, not one rider's missed their slot, even with the drizzle."

Osur pointed at the puddles. "You call this a drizzle?"

"If we shut down now," Seb said, "that's going to be... oh... about sixty disappointed customers."

"With legitimate complaints to the town board, and all the time in the world to lodge them," Lauren added.

Osur sighed. "Can't you push it all back into Sunday?"

"Sunday's booked solid, too," Lauren said. It wasn't, but Osur didn't need to know.

Chuck slunk back beside them. "And remember," he said, "these are hovercrafts. They're just as safe in rain as in dry."

"Maybe even safer," Seb added. "Heavier and less prone to drift."

Osur panned across the crowd, heartily engrossed in the soggy hijinks, and shrugged in rank surrender. "If anybody gets hurt, it'll be your three keisters prone to drift—to court." He trudged back towards the fairgrounds.

Seb held the list to his lips and blew across it, as if it were a smoking gun and he an expert marksman. Chuck said, "I'll be damned."

"A broken clock's still right twice a day," Lauren said. "Don't let it go to your head."

The hovercrafts screeched towards the finish. She waved the checkered flag and cried, "Five-thirty flat! Now, we're cooking with fire!"

Morning leached towards muggy noon. The hovercrafts, resplendent in their lacquer glaze, droned the course heroically. In their wake flowed a steady stream of green, filling up the money box. Now and then, when no one was looking, Seb would plunge his hand through the cash and wiggle his fingers excitedly. It felt, a little, like the fine balsa wood of his dad's or Timmy's vintage Dreamin'. But most of all, it felt like victory.

The rain subsided. Patches of blue played peek-a-boo

behind the leaden clouds. The prepaid racers came and went, grateful that they'd braved the rains and left before the afternoon. A vengeful sun soared overhead, baking the asphalt puddles to steam. A glut of new faces thronged the queue. And they looked miserable.

"It's happening again," Lauren said. "See?"

As they had the previous day, people were steadily leaving the line, grumbling and grousing as they departed, dragging belligerent children behind. Those who remained were dripping with sweat, some even dropping to bended knees. The paramedics scurried about, offering towels and cold water bottles, but the writing on the wall was clear.

"Why didn't we think to sell afternoon time slots?" Seb said. "And where the hell is Chuck?"

Chuck had gone to use the restroom, but that had been fifteen minutes ago.

"Montezuma's revenge," Lauren said. "And I still say we did the right thing. This can't seem too exclusive."

"Yeah, but—"

"Ugh!" A woman murmured, staggering into a paramedic's arms. The crowd and queued riders gasped. The paramedic helped her towards the ambulance.

Seb and Lauren hurriedly loaded the next two riders in queue: Joey and Pat, the town's two highest-ranking Cub Scouts, who both excelled and competed at everything. "Let 'er rip!" Lauren said, and waved the checkered flag.

They motored off in clouds of smoke. The backdraft from the engines made the air, momentarily, feel like even more of a sauna. The crowd could take only so much of this heat. They were all on borrowed time.

"Crap," Seb said. A police ATV was speeding uphill. He'd never discount the importance of safety. But victory was just so close. "Got any ideas?" he asked Lauren.

"Where's Chuck when you need him?" she said. "Only pathetic groveling is going to save our bacon now."

The police cycle pulled beside them. He recognized its rider: Officer Rose, the town K-9 cop.

"Eric," Lauren giggled, batting her eyes. "Come to join the fun? A hovercraft-ATV race *would* be a great conversation piece."

He pulled off his helmet. "Black flag, kids. Mr. Osur sent me. He'd have come himself but it's just too darn hot."

"You can't shut us down now," Seb protested. "Things are just getting interesting. Look!" He pointed to Tomba's Twist. "Pat and Joey are butting heads at something new."

"Overachievers," Rose said. "But seriously," he raised his voice, "time to put this on ice."

The queued adults moaned ecstatically, much to the chagrin of their grumbling children. The irony was blatant: Seb would have kicked himself if he could. They'd been so fixated on morning rains they'd failed to anticipate afternoon heat and what to do about it.

"It won't be all day," Rose said, "probably only an hour or two."

But an hour or two, or even less, would deal his hopes a death-blow. The coffers were healthy, to be sure, but they'd spent so much on lacquer and bags, not to mention extra gasoline, they'd only just started climbing back into black.

"What if we shortened the line," Lauren said, "and moved it back inside the hangar?"

"It's just as steamy and hot under there. And by the looks of all these folks, they're getting ready to ditch anyway, and nothing's going to keep them here. So shut it down—"

"Did somebody say, *time to put this on ice?*" a familiar voice cried out.

A clunky old minivan engine rumbled, followed by the ding-a-ling of frozen treats for sale. A lusty cheer burst from the crowd. Over it, the voice cried out, "Thought I'd show some spunk of my own!"

Lauren's jaw dropped. "He didn't."

Seb turned.

He *had*.

Cresting the hill was an ice cream truck. And riding shotgun inside it was Chuck.

He leaned out the window. "This isn't all," he shouted, pointing behind. "Look!"

In tow, climbing up the hill, was a knot of circus performers: juggler, magician, comedian, fire-eater, and even a live falcon trainer, all to entertain the crowds.

Seb's heart leapt. His aspirations, of late so gray, burst into Technicolor. Chuck had come through for him again, without having even been asked. Pythias had nothing on him. Even Lauren had to smirk. "I don't impress easy," she said, "but *damn*."

The truck lurched to a stop. Like flies upon a juicy steak, the parched and hungry crowd thronged about it. The circus performers strode to and fro, turning tricks for the queued racers, whose eyes now beamed delighted smiles.

Seb flashed Chuck a double thumbs-up. "Genius," he said, "pure genius."

Chuck jumped from the cab. "Oh, it was nothing. I just did what I thought you'd do."

Officer Rose shook his head. "You kids have nine lives. Which is great because I have more to say."

Seb steeled himself. Cryptic warnings like that were seldom good news.

"Tomorrow," Rose said, "now they're telling me, there's a last-minute addition. Some up-and-coming R&B group... P.M. Dawn, I think they're called. We can't hold a concert with all this noise and they need an open space for the crowd."

Seb held his breath, head swimming. He could see Lauren and Chuck doing the same. Rose said, "So the town wants you finished and cleared out by noon."

Seb released his breath. "Is that all?" It was hardly ideal

but not fatal. At the rate their coffers were filling today, tomorrow was shaping up to be gravy, anyway.

"I hope that's not too much of a downer," Rose said. "I hate being the bearer of bad news. Kids are my weakness— especially kids who want to be cops."

It seemed a bizarre but sincere admission. Lauren shrugged and said, "We'll deal."

Rose said, "Splendid. Now, about that hovercraft-ATV race—?"

"Stop it! *Stop it!* Get off of me!"

Panicked screams rent the mirth, from the direction of the Corn Maze.

"Get off. *Get off!* No!"

"What the hell?" Seb said. He, Chuck, and Lauren ran towards the noise, Rose following behind.

Beside the defunct Corn Maze entrance, Joey and Pat were standing alone. "They stole our rides," Pat said.

As if Seb didn't know. "Who?"

Joey pointed.

Across the course, on the back straightaway, Cain and Mabel were hurtling top-speed towards each other, Rob and Aloysius piloting them.

xxii.

LIKE A FAST-EXSANGUINATING patient, Seb and Lauren wheeled Cain into the hangar bay. Seb could still hear the horrible din of the crash, echoing in his ears like a death-rattle.

"We'll fix him," Lauren said, "I'm sure. The skirt's intact and we have enough wood. It's going to be fine, trust me." But her face told a different story.

Chuck burst through the doors. "How bad?"

"Bad," Seb said. "Switch to single-rider." Chuck spun away, volunteers in tow.

The wail of a police car siren, no doubt containing Aloysius and Rob, faded into the distance. But that was meaningless now. The damage had been done.

He stared at the carnage. Of the collision, Mabel had gotten the better, by far. Aside from a few scratches, she was still operational. But Cain had not been nearly so lucky. The impact had shredded its front hover-pod, shattering its frame and air-pipes, and denting its engine on several sides. The skirt was, miraculously, largely undamaged, but that was about the only good news. It was eerily, horribly reminiscent of his dad's and Timmy's mangled airplanes. "Déjà fucking vu," he said. The Dreamin' had never seemed farther away.

Afternoon raced into the ether. Mabel's droning near, then far, bonded into a regular backbeat, from which Seb counted the passage of hours. Lauren and Seb worked like beavers: measuring, cutting, and sanding wood, cobbling a new Cain from the ruins of the old. The crowd, though smaller, made up for its size, cheering emphatically for the lone riders. Chuck, periodically, popped in to check and offer words of encouragement. Lauren whistled and cracked silly jokes. But in his heart Seb knew they were screwed. If Cain couldn't give them a morning of racing, they might as well throw in the towel.

A warm, sultry evening fell, replacing the warmer, sultrier day. The Jubilee-goers had long left for home. A hush crept over the racecourse and hangar, nettled only, here and there, by toads hunting mosquitoes in the dark.

Seb tightened the bolts on Cain's engine-mount, then wiped his hands and exhaled, "Done."

Chuck relocked the money box. "One thousand and fifty dollars," he said, "including yesterday's."

Seb did some rapid calculations. Single-rider had kept them afloat, but they were still in dire straits. With debt and tomorrow's half-day limit, they'd have to be fast and nearly flawless, and even then, they'd need some luck. "We promised we'd reopen the Corn Maze tomorrow. That's two or three fewer races per hour."

"We could always renege," Chuck said. "Who'd blame us?"

Lauren, head in her hands, said, "Or up the fee."

Chuck said, "But you said—"

"I know. It's tacky but there's just one day left. We make a cash prize, like half the day's earnings. People will at least feel they're paying into something."

"If we even *can* race," Chuck said. "Seb?"

The moment of truth had come. Cain was rebuilt, lacquered, and painted. Its pipes had all been patched or replaced, and the engine reinstalled. But hovercrafts were finicky souls. Hitting the sweet spots with balance and airflow was an art, not science. "I guess we're about to find out," Seb said.

The three of them clustered, holding hands, trying to summon whatever good luck could still be wrung from a fickle universe. They chanted in unison, "Work, work, work..."

Seb tugged the engine's starter-cord. The friction felt greater than it had before. He pulled it hard. The engine spun but didn't turn over.

"Work, work, *work*..."

He tried again.

Nothing.

"Work, *work, work*..."

He propped his foot against Cain for more leverage, and ripped another try. The engine swirled and popped once or twice, but ground to an ignominious halt.

Chuck and Lauren gritted their teeth, trying to disguise their fear, but Seb could see straight through the ruse. What they were feeling, he felt more. He spat on his palms and rolled them in sawdust. They'd come too far to fizzle like this. He clutched his fingers around the handle, so hard his knuckles strained blue-white, then filled his lungs and snarled aloud, and yanked the cord with all his strength. "*Work!*"

The engine sputtered, then sprang to life.

Lauren and Chuck together cried, "Yeah!"

"Yes!" Seb said, "Yes! *Yes!*"

The three of them danced across the hangar, to the beat of Cain's whining engine. Once again—somehow, some way—they'd snatched victory from the jaws of defeat. The races, after all, would resume. The dream was still alive. The Dreamin' would still be—

Glugglugglugglugglugglug....

The engine gurgled, coughed, and popped, then made

a hideous clanking sound, like a brick trapped in a washing machine.

"Oh, that can't be good," Chuck said.

Seb froze in place mid-moonwalk. The engine belched a cloud of smoke, then spit bolts across the room and rattled into silence. A noxious, oily smell wafted up. "Shit," Seb said. The engine was leaking. He grabbed a rag and reached out to sop it—

"No!" Lauren grabbed his hand away.

Flames shimmied up, then burst from the engine. Chuck lunged for a fire extinguisher, and sprayed its contents all over Cain. The flames dissipated, leaving a charred-over husk of an engine.

Lauren opened the hangar door, waving out the smoke and fumes. Chuck unleashed a stream of invectives such as Seb had never heard and would have, in a different place, brought a mouthful of soap. Seb could only stand and stare in anguished disbelief. Clearly, he'd missed a step or two. The extent of the engine's interior damage hadn't been apparent, or he hadn't bothered to look closely enough. But it was entirely moot now. There was no escaping the obvious.

The universe hated Sebastian Riggs.

"Easy fix," Chuck said, his unhinged sanguinity beginning to grate.

"Sure," Seb said, "if you're John DeLorean."

"So we find a mechanic," Chuck said.

Lauren said, "At ten o'clock on a Saturday?"

"No," Chuck said, "first thing tomorrow."

"This is Bergen County," she said. "Good luck finding *anything* open Sunday."

"Or anyone willing to come here," Seb said. "And I clearly know dick about engines, but I'm guessing this is no quick fix."

"It's toast," Lauren said. "Literally." Her implacable aura of moxie shattered. A grimace crept across her face. She threw her arms above her head and stormed off towards the hangar door.

Seb said, "Where are you going?"

"I can't," she said, "I just can't."

Chuck took a perfunctory step in pursuit, but she'd already vanished out into the night. The ship was sinking fast. Seb would never have guessed she'd be first rat overboard.

"At first light," Chuck said, "we buy a new one. You can use my share of the dough."

Chuck's chivalry was true, dwarfed only by his naïveté. "If we could *find* a Briggs & Stratton five horsepower engine," Seb said, "remember, it has to be same as Mabel's, it would take a lot more than just your share. And it'd waste at least another hour fitting it into Cain. But thank you."

"Anything to help," Chuck said.

A sense of fate washed over Seb. The time had come, at longest last, to finally give up the ghost. His dream was utterly, exhaustively dead; no Miracle Max could revive it anew. No one could have tried harder nor striven more valiantly. He hadn't failed; he'd just run out of time. "I know you would," Seb answered. *That,* if anything, would have to be the gold at the end of an otherwise forlorn rainbow.

Evening, to the tune of frogs and mockingbirds in distant hills, waxed later, cooler, and ever darker. Midnight, like a stealthy thief, came and went unnoticed. Seb and Chuck, both well past exhaustion, lounged on boxes in the hangar, regaling each other with tales of their youth, remembered well but better embellished; by and by trading bawdy riddles, each trying to one-up the other.

"No, no," Chuck said. "Kelly LeBrock over Samantha Fox."

"*Weird Science* Kelly LeBrock, or that shampoo commercial?" Seb said. "And I'd take Robin Givens over either of them any day."

"Mike Tyson might take umbrage."

Seb picked up one of Cain's engine's bolts and lobbed it high across the hangar into a wastepaper basket. "Magic scores from downtown," he said. "And I beat *Punch-Out* my first try, remember?"

Seb couldn't help but smile. *Mike Tyson's Punch-Out.* He and Chuck had stayed up late playing that and *Super Mario Brothers,* then watching *Little Shop of Horrors* on HBO until they could fend off fatigue no more. Sixth grade hadn't been all terrible, in spite of Rob and Aloysius. He'd discovered world history and a love of Old Testament stories. He'd watched the U.S. return to the stars with the launch of space shuttle *Discovery,* and marveled at the tortuous intrigue of a presidential election. Against all odds, he'd built hovercrafts and etched his place in Stony Glen lore, even if he'd not quite reached Lloyd Llewellyn's rarified air. Life was good enough. Really, life was actually pretty good.

But the Dreamin' would have made it better. And that, in the end, was the tragedy.

"It would've been sweet," Seb said. "Seeing the looks on their faces."

"Look at the bright side," Chuck said, divvying up their two-days' earnings. "Even if it's not three hundred, you're closer than you were before." He handed Seb two hundred and thirty-three dollars. "That's something to be damn proud of. In no time you can earn the rest."

The thought of saddling up again, only to have the next quixotic get-rich-quick scheme shot out from underneath him, rankled like a woolen sweater on the Fourth of July. Seb, Inc. was done. *Seb* was done. The rest of his life ahead of him beckoned. "Nah," he said, "you know how it is. Back to school in less than two weeks. Then it's homework, shorter days, TV actually worth watching. Maybe I'll join the A-V club, turn some of these dreams of mine into stories. Hell knows I've been doing enough dreaming this summer." He laughed aloud to himself. "Dreamin' in eighty-nine."

Outside, a vehicle approached, followed by a knock on the door. Chuck said, "Lauren, come to grovel?"

Lauren had given Seb's dream her best. She had nothing to grovel for. "She wouldn't knock," Seb said, staggering to his feet. "Guess again."

"McGyver, hopefully," Chuck said. "He's about our only hope."

"Sadly true," Seb said. But it didn't matter anymore. Seb, at last, had found his peace. He opened the door.

It *was* Lauren. And next to her was Timmy.

xxiii.

SEB STUMBLED, flinching up his guard. The last time he'd seen Timmy, he was burying his fist inside Seb's gut and stealing his hard-earned cash. He turned to Lauren. "You brought *him?*"

"I can't help who answers my distress flares," she said.

Chuck rushed to Seb's side. "Get the hell out of Dodge."

"All in good time, schmuck," Timmy said. "Business first."

In the splotchy light from the exit sign, Seb could see that both Timmy's eyes were black-and-blue. He couldn't help but feel pity, and hated that he did. "Business?" Seb said. "What do you want?"

"Oh, *you* know," Timmy said, in his best Jack Nicolson's Joker. "A little song and dance, and then your head upon a–"

"*What do you want?*" Seb grabbed him with both hands. "You've wasted enough of my youth."

Timmy peeled Seb's hands off his collar. "It's no picnic for me either." He propped the door wide with a cinderblock, then vanished into the steamy darkness.

Chuck said, "What's his game?"

In his wearied fugue, Seb could swear he was dreaming. Everything Timmy did was for Timmy. This was the last thing he'd have expected. He said, "No idea."

Lauren said, "Just watch."

Timmy's golf cart whirred into view. Seb's heart leapt: it was past inconceivable. Hitched to the cart was one of Timmy's lawnmowers. And its engine was a five horsepower Briggs & Stratton.

Timmy backed it through the door, then unhitched the tow-ball. The lawnmower, in neutral, rolled beside Cain, almost as if it knew its fate. Seb shook his head: there was no doubt at all. He *had* to be dreaming.

"I'll pour the Mountain Dew," Lauren said, and skipped into the hangar bay.

Seb and Chuck could only stare. In a single, fell, bewildering swoop, their tragedy was triumph—maybe. There was still a morning of racing ahead, and no guarantees. But, at least, they'd get to try.

"Make sure you mix enough oil in," Timmy said. He climbed back into his cart. "I'd also replace the spark plugs. My father and my brothers..." He touched his bruised face, wincing. "They have certain ideas. And now, thanks to you, I have different ones." He drove off into the night.

Seb looked at Chuck. "Pinch me?"

Chuck said, "I was going to ask you the same thing."

Seb spit on his palms and rubbed them together, then grabbed a wrench and ratchet. His date with destiny beckoned. The dream was alive and kicking.

*   *   *   *   *

The metal door rolled overhead, to the roar of an ecstatic crowd. Seb, Chuck, and Lauren, wiry after a full night's toil, fueled by Mountain Dew and will, squinted in the morning sun, leading Mabel and the rebuilt Cain to the starting line. The atmosphere was electric. It was do-or-die with no time to waste.

"As many of you know," Seb said, "we said today would be a race-off and that we'd open the Corn Maze back up." The crowd hooted its approval. Officer Rose stood nearby, arms folded: every minute this morning was being watched. "But sadly," Seb said, "we have less than five hours, so we don't really have much choice. We'll race head-to-head for bragging rights. Best time by when they shut us down wins you half today's earnings, plus a nice certificate."

"Suitable for framing," Lauren added.

"Nothing but the best," Seb said. His prestige, though, was about to nose-dive. "However, please note a significant change." Over the placard touting five-dollar races, he plastered one that read eight dollars.

A sullen grumble, soft but rising, simmered from the crowd. "A fifty-plus percent hike?" one called. "What the hell is that?"

Chuck said, "We had some trouble yesterday."

"Yeah, we remember," another said. "What, are you collecting for those hooligans' bail?" The grumbles gelled into a boo, as people started drifting away.

Lauren stepped into the crowd. "Hold on, wait up, excuse me," she said. The drifters halted in their tracks. The others parted as she passed. "I want you all to know," she said, "this wasn't how we envisioned this. It looked for a while like today wouldn't happen, but my good friend Seb just wouldn't give up."

She smiled at him. All eyes swung his way, but all Seb could see was the numeral *thirty*, the magical number of races needed to make this day a success, and even then, by the skin of their teeth. That—and fireworks, bursting in his eyes, thanks to Lauren's praise.

"This dream of his," she went on, "it's bigger than him, it's bigger than me, and it's big enough to hold all of *you*. He has no quit inside him. He wouldn't know failure if it up and bit him, whether or not he can see that himself. So, let's help make his dream come true. Let's all dream together. No matter what, *I'm in*." She slapped down sixteen dollars. "That's for me and some sad sap who's about to have his or her butt kicked. All that remains to be seen is *who*." She spread her arms. "Any takers?"

Her spunk was an ambrosial elixir. Swooning, Seb grabbed ahold of himself. If love was a verb, then lovers could only be people of action. "Please," he said, "you're all racing for second," and dropped sixteen dollars of his own. "Who's *my* first victim?" They both stared hard at Chuck.

"Don't look at me," Chuck said. "I think you're both nuts."

They glared harder. Chuck said, "Seriously?"

Lauren glowered with such brio Seb could swear her face might catch flame.

"Fine," Chuck said, and waved his cash. "Who thinks they can take the Chuckster?"

Wearing varsity team T-shirts, a group of Hawthorn High School kids stepped out of the crowd and threw down a gauntlet, followed as they were, in turn, by kids from as far away as north Rockland, and even Don Bosco and Bergen Catholic. Word, it seems, had traveled well, and competition would be fierce. But the real race, Seb knew, was against the clock. At twelve o'clock noon—twelve-thirty latest—the town would push them aside for the concert. There was nothing to do but seize the morning. "May the best man win," Seb said.

Lauren strapped herself into Mabel. "The best man," she said, "is a woman."

She turned the key; the hovercrafts roared, their push-vents whirring and skirts inflating, then trundled to the starting line. The crowd began to clap in time, slowly, then with greater verve, until the air was filled with glee and the ground beneath them shook. Chuck held up the checkered flag. Seb, with stopwatch, mounted the ladder.

Lauren adjusted her helmet and goggles. "I'll spot you fifty yards there, champ," she said to her deer-in-the-headlights opponent, "just so you know we're all on the level."

Cain bobbled down the straightaway, stopping fifty yards away. The crowd's cheers reached a fever pitch. Chuck reassuringly slapped Seb's back. "Lloyd Llewellyn's got nothing on us." He raised aloft the checkered flag. "Three...two...one," he hollered, "*Go!*"

The hovercrafts hightailed away, to the viewers' adulation, into the thick of the homemade gauntlet and deeper, still, into Stony Glen lore.

As if atoning for yesterday's rain, the August sun shone twice as bright, tempered by a northeast breeze, dropping the mercury but buoying spirits on this, the Day of Judgment. The queue, in no time, stretched downhill. Beside it, vendors set up shop and troupers plied their trades, showing off for laughs and tips. The crowd, refreshed and entertained, thumped and waved oaktag placards, playfully hailing the dauntless racers like Greens and Blues of Constantinople, as old Cornball had taught them. Most knew they'd never get to race, so long was the queue and so short the hours, but for their cheers one'd never know.

Chuck, like a demon lollipop man, loaded, saw off, then unloaded racers with a rhythm that shamed even yesterday's pace, itself a study in speed and finesse. His own match-pairing had not gone well, eating some Catholic school girl's dust and failing to get her phone number after. Lauren, in contrast, had smoked both the course and her hapless opponent; sitting pretty all morning, watching all comers fall. But Seb, like a cashier, could see only numbers, ticking away at a vigorous clip but never quite vigorous enough. He checked his watch: it was pushing 12:20 p.m. Five hours had vanished inside a twinkling. The magic number now was four. At the rate they'd been going, they'd never reach it, as drop-dead time was 12:30 p.m. He needed to steal fifteen minutes. The question was, *from who?*

From the sidelines, Officer Rose looked on solemnly. The germ of a notion began to flicker. What was it Lauren had admonished Seb? *You learn more by listening than by talking?* Beneath that façade, Rose harbored a weakness. A chance was Seb's to seize.

He grabbed Lauren's hand and squirmed through the crowd, locating Mr. Schultz's grandkids. He pulled a Milky Way from his pocket, the last that remained of last night's victuals. "Hey," he said, and gathered them close. "I have another job for you."

*　　　　*　　　　*　　　　*　　　　*

Seb ran with all speed across the fairgrounds, towards the town's command kiosk. In the distance, behind him, he could hear Mabel's din: another race had been seen off. The magic number, now, was three. His margin for error was zero. The plan would work, or they'd fall short. For surety's sake, Chuck had been left out; his loading skills vastly exceeded his play-acting, anyhow. The others had been fully briefed. For a hip-pocket ruse it was merely average, probably not worthy of *Three's Company*. But all he needed was fifteen minutes. In the fog of war, all bets were off.

Like drones rushing off a toppled anthill, the towns-people, vendors, and performers scurried, lowering tents and boxing up wares, in anticipation, no doubt, of the coming concert. In the midst of the chaos, looking his age, Seb found the redoubtable old soldier. "Mr. Osur," Seb said, cheerily, "Officer Rose wanted to know if drop-dead time's still 12:30 p.m."

Osur, sorting raffle tickets, replied, "Why wouldn't it be?"

Seb shrugged. "Far be it from me to question a cop."

The old man raised a skeptical eyebrow and grabbed a walkie-talkie. "Rose, come in, come in," he said. From the opposite side came crackling static, punctuated, here and there, by what sounded vaguely like giggling boys. "Officer Rose, *come in.*"

The garbled childish voice replied, "Mahoney here. Come in, Tackleberry."

Osur rolled his eyes. "Radio's on the fritz," he said. "Perfect."

Time for the kill-shot. Seb said, "I think all he needs is a simple thumbs-up. Look..." He pointed uphill to the racing grounds. "You can see him from here, and he can see you."

Charlotte, the town pool tag-checker-cum-theater cashier, barged beside them. "Sarge," she said, "they need you poolside. Something about an escaped circus seal."

Osur groaned, "Even MacKelvie wasn't this useless," and staggered to his feet.

"Wait," Seb said, "don't forget about Rose."

Osur mumbled, "Another genius." He turned and waved his arms about until he'd gotten Rose's attention. Then he flashed a stern thumb's-up and scampered off in the town pool's direction.

Charlotte turned to Seb, scowling. "Young love let you down yet, son?"

It was a deep question, dwarfed only by its inappropriateness. But for all his newfound armor of cynicism, love hadn't added any plates to that suit. Love, in fact, had removed a few. Lauren had removed them. "Not on your life," he said, and spun away, hoofing it back towards the racecourse.

*   *   *   *   *

"And for the last time, at least *this* year," Chuck bellowed, "three...two...one... Go, go, *go!*" He waved, then dropped, the checkered flag, then twirled it like a majorette.

Seb slowed to a walk nearing the starting line. His watch

read 12:47 p.m. Lauren was waiting with ear-to-ear grin. Seb took a knee, panting; two nights without sleep had finally caught up. In the distance, for the sudden silence, he could tell Cain and Mabel had entered the wind shaft. The roars of the crowd were fervent as ever, grateful for three bonus races, but tinged, as they seemed, with regret for the end. The Schultz kids ran about helter-skelter, fighting over Officer Rose's police hat and radio, pressing buttons and cranking knobs, raising a shrill cacophony.

"Guys," Rose said, "I really need my walkie back. What if someone important is calling?"

Lauren said, "Imagine that."

The throaty rolls of the hovercrafts' engines split the air for the very last time, bursting from the Corn Maze and thundering down the home straightaway. Seb could feel his heart take flight. For some, the sound of a dream come true was a newborn's cry, or a shared *I do*, or *Pomp and Circumstance*. But for Seb the sound of sweet success was none other than the choppy roar of a five-horsepower Briggs & Stratton, followed by the vinyl whoosh of hovercraft skirts speeding hence.

"You kids really *do* have nine lives," Rose said. "I can't believe Osur gave thumbs-up on the extra fifteen minutes."

"Eh," Seb said, "what's a quarter-hour between friends?"

Cain and Mabel, side by splendid, homegrown side, buzzed across the finish line. The crowd released a primal scream. Chuck raised the money box high overhead, as if he'd won the Stanley Cup. Lauren, whose time had stood all day, climbed atop the lookout ladder and stage-dived into her adoring public, followed in swift succession by Chuck.

Thirty races up, then down—and just like that, it was history. Seb had won. *They* had won. Lauren's preposterous, absurd scheme, against all odds and defying all logic, had borne the sweetest, richest fruit. Their three-day haul was three hundred dollars each, and maybe even a smidge more.

Seb's dream had come true.

The Dreamin' was his.

Seb could only bask in the moment. Maybe the universe *didn't* hate him.

Old Mr. Osur, silent as death, sidled next to him. Seb couldn't resist an impish grin. "You caught that seal, I hope," he said.

"Oversized muskrat, it seems," Osur said. "And you swindled me again, kid. I get the feeling you enjoy it."

Indeed, he did. "Not a chance, sir." But from here on out, he'd be arrow-straight.

"That's swell," Osur said. "When I make you three honorary Town Fathers, you can look me in the eye." He shook Seb's hand and walked away, then stopped and turned around. "Oh, and I like my grass cut long...next summer, when I hire you back."

Seb laughed to himself. Seb, Inc. was dead, never to return. But the day was young—and beautiful. Flowing past atop the crowd, Chuck said, "Surf's up, dude."

"Welcome aboard," Lauren said, grabbing his collar and pulling him along.

"Cowabunga!" Seb cried. It seemed the perfect metaphor. At all points, he'd been held up by others. He could never have come this far alone. "Put your hands together for Chuck," he said, "a pit boss' pit boss." The crowd applauded; Chuck pumped his fists. "And let's hear it once and again for Lauren, today's champion."

The crowd wailed in veneration. "You like me," she cooed, "you really like me!"

"Force of nature," Chuck said, "just like prickly heat."

Or a supernova. Seb took the money box from Chuck. "Your certificate," he said, "is up to you, seeing as how *you* were going to design it." The crowd laughed. He peeled out two hundred and twenty-five dollars, half the day's earnings, adjusted for gas. "But I'm proud to present you with this,"

Seb said. "I'm proud to call you my friend." He reached out and took hold of Lauren's and Chuck's hands. "Both of you." The crowd crowed its approval.

"Hold on," Lauren said, "not so fast. You there." She motioned towards Kelli, Mabel's very first competition pilot, who'd dutifully ridden and watched all three days. "Here you go, squirt," she said, and handed Kelli her winnings. "Do something nice for yourself, you hear me?"

Kelli's mouth quivered as she took the gift. She tried, it looked, to mutter "thank you," but couldn't quite seem to squeeze out the words past her verklempt gratitude. But words were superfluous. Everyone knew.

"Let's hear it for our champion!" The crowd, *sans* a dry eye, whooped and hollered the loudest so far, then unloaded Lauren, Seb, and Chuck. Without being asked, all spectators spread out and began to take down and load bales of hay into Harold's Farm trucks. Like royal bearers with priceless crown jewels, the high school racing teams carried Cain and Mabel into the hangar. In mere moments, the race-course was gone, the concert venue rising.

"I could get used to this kind of service," Seb said. "I wonder if they hire out for homework?"

"That was two hundred and twenty-five bucks," Chuck said to Lauren. "Are you that insane?"

"Eh," she said, "I had an unfair advantage. And, anyway, I got the *real* prize." She squared up face-to-face with Seb and pressed her mouth against his own.

The world burst into vibrant colors, as if a secret, hidden door, lost for ages but whispered about, had finally been unlocked. In warmth a furnace, in smell lavender, in taste a cornucopia, this, the way that angels love, had now, at long last, called Seb home. He could feel his soul, among other things, soar. A pioneer on distant shore, nothing would ever compare to this, his twelve-year-old innocence seeping away the longer he and Lauren sucked face.

"Ugh," Chuck said, "could you two be any more disgusting?"

Chuck had given Seb his all, when least he had deserved it. If not for Chuck, as much as Lauren, Seb wouldn't have had three hundred dollars in hand. "I don't know about her," Seb said, "but *I* sure as hell can." He grabbed Chuck by his shoulders and planted a juicy kiss on his cheek.

"*Ew,*" Chuck shouted, "Gross!" He ran off retching. "Friggin' pervert. Gross!"

"You love me," Seb called after him.

"Yeah, yeah," Chuck said. "Call me when the Dreamin' comes. I'll be boning up my R/C skills." He disappeared into the swarming fairgrounds.

"A strange little man," Lauren said. She placed her hands around Seb's hips. "Make out under the bleachers?"

Nothing could have sounded more heavenly. He reached in his pocket to stuff in his cash, then realized it was occupied. There was something important that Seb had to do, and it couldn't wait. And Lauren didn't have to know. "Sorry," he said, "I've got a date with the sandman. Raincheck, if you please?"

"Hmm," she said, "you're lucky you're cute. I'll catch you on the flip, Sebastian. Seems you can't tie your shoes without me."

He kissed her on her forehead, then turned and raced back towards his street.

xxiv.

ASHY LARRY'S HOUSE was still, save for the pings of falling acorns against his tinny shed roof. Seb crept round his backyard porch. As it had been weeks before, the door was strangely ajar. For a once-wealthy man, Larry knew dick about security. He creaked the door wider and slipped inside. Decorum would've dictated he ring the doorbell, but the scene he'd found was fishy at least. And Lauren's kiss lingered on his lips, so all systems were in overdrive.

The house was its usual unholy sauna. Seb lowered the thermostat as he passed, then sucked in apprehensive breath. Sooner or later, one of these nights, Larry would melt himself out of existence, like the Wicked Witch of the West. But not today: Seb let go his breath. He could hear Larry moving inside.

He stepped into the bedroom. Larry was lying awake in his bed, thumbing through old photo albums. "Casa mia è casa tua, Sebastian," he said. "What, you forget how to knock?"

"I figured you'd, um, be asleep," Seb said. He had to focus on not saying *dead*.

"I figured *you'd* be by now," Larry said. "I heard about the hovercrafts. You must be very proud—and tired."

Tired didn't even begin to describe it. "Yeah, well..." Seb reached into his pocket. "I have something to show you and it couldn't wait. Trust me, you'll be glad I did." He pulled out the photo scrap from Lloyd Llewellyn's time capsule. "I believe you know what this is?"

The old man took the scap. His crinkled eyes quickened; he drew choppy breath. Seb said, "Flip it around."

With quivering hands, he turned it over, then strained to read the old handwriting. Exposition was unnecessary. He knew exactly what it was. "What was lost is found," Seb said. "Now you can find some peace, I'd say. And, hopefully, so can Brent."

Larry beamed through glistening eyes. "I can't wait to visit him tomorrow." He laughed, "He was always the brains between us, you know." He pressed the photo to his breast. "What—or *who*—is right beside you really is what matters. Truer words were never spoken, Sebastian. It's no dumb luck that *you* found this."

It would've been easy to dismiss out of hand. But somehow, now, Seb wasn't so sure. "I think maybe you're right," he said. "But all I did was bring it home."

He thanked Larry for all he'd done, then tucked him in and slipped outside. The quest that began more than fifty years prior was finally consigned to history. He and Chuck were Larry and Brent. The poetry of life had rhymed.

As it had in the movie theater lobby, the fluffy pink cloud of his fancy returned. There was nothing to do but climb aboard, as *Love Boat's* theme each Thursday night urged, and set a course for adventure. "Weigh anchor," he commanded.

The cloud took flight above Stony Glen. Like Blanchard atop a nascent New Jersey, nigh two hundred years before, from his eagle-eyed vantage, Seb could see the shape of his world as if it were a living map. His summer's production— part comedy, but mostly tragedy—had played out here, among these nooks, as many, no doubt, had done before and would until the cracks of doom. Like Lloyd Llewellyn, perhaps someday, his quest in the Summer of '89 would be the stuff of campfire tales and legends passed down from father to son like musty, well-worn heirlooms. Or, in no time, the world would forget. But *he* could never forget.

Before he knew it, and not entirely sure how, he'd arrived in his bedroom. Kit was fast asleep already, clutching her stuffed animals. Seb dropped his cash into his jar, placed trophy-like beside his bed, and scrambled into his pajamas. First thing tomorrow, hand-in-hand with Lauren, he'd trade it for a cashier's check. Then it'd be off to *R/C Modeler*, and into the annals of destiny.

He plopped upon his still-unmade bed and buried his face in his pillow. Sleep took him whole without a fight and sped him off to punchy dreams: of Larry and Brent and Llewellyn's time capsule, of hovercrafts and vanquished foes, of Chuck and the Dreamin'—but mostly, of Lauren. Lucid, he could soar on angels' wings and command her every emotion. But then he remembered he didn't have to.

The dreams faded into oblivion. The racket of hammers and whirring drills roused Seb into daylight. It sounded like a dear old friend; the rugged music of his father's craft before tragedy had silenced it, like life returning to normal. Not just normal.

Great.

He turned to admire his earnings.

His money jar was empty.

XXV.

SEB'S BLOOD RAN COLD. The thought was too
terrible even to fathom. But the sounds of construction,
plus missing money, could mean only one thing.

He stormed into the kitchen. As if he'd been expecting
it, Rich, his father, was standing, arms crossed. Rich mas-
saged his mangled hand, then glared hard at his son. Certain
he already knew the answer, Seb demanded, "What did
you do?"

"What you should've done," Rich said.

"Says you."

Rich nodded. "You had every chance."

He'd been warned about this very thing. *Parents,* Lauren's
wisdom echoed. *They're just making it up as they go, like you and
me. The trick is knowing when they're right and when it's you who's
right.* She'd been more prescient than she could've known.
But this was miles beyond the pale. Seb said, "Where's my
money?"

"*Your* money?"

"You're damn right *my* money."

"Watch your language," Rich said. "What's yours belongs
to me. You're twelve years old, Sebastian. What could you
ever need it for? Comics?"

Seb said, "I earned it."

"And your family thanks you." Rich pointed to the ceiling hole, where a crew was framing the upstairs addition. "Priorities, Sebastian. I'd thought you'd have seen that yourself. Another failure on my part, I guess."

That was a cop-out, and a weak one. Seb said, "So you stole it?"

Rich held up his injured hand. "Didn't leave me much choice, did you?"

It was the same shit Timmy had pulled with Seb, and he, in turn, had laid on Chuck. It had to be someone else's fault; go blame someone else. If only you hadn't demanded fair treatment, I wouldn't have had to lay you to waste. Weeks ago, even, it would've made hay. But it was just that kind of spinelessness that had sped him to the foot of all pecking-orders. And now, his own father had robbed him. "Yes."

Rich said, "Yes?"

Seb leaned into his father's face. "I'm done feeling bad about your hand. That injury wasn't a blank check for you. It's too bad what happened but I earned that money."

"Then consider it a hospitality tax," Rich said. "The upstairs is for all of us. It's time you started pulling your weight." He patted Seb's shoulder dismissively and turned to leave. "We're done here."

But Seb wasn't finished, not by damn sight. After every gauntlet and travail crossed—some self-imposed, some others not—the thought of falling on his sword again gnawed like poison sumac. He said, "You owe me, dad."

His father said, "Oh, I owe *you?* Consider that account paid in full, then, Seb. You have air in your lungs and food on your plate and, now, a roof above your head. My own father—"

"I don't give a shit." He'd heard that lecture many times, and it didn't justify theft. "Give me back my money *now.*"

"*Me,*" Rich said, "always me, me, *me.* Did it ever cross your spoiled mind there are bigger things than model planes? You've been seeing too much of that kid Charles. This household doesn't live off alimony. We have priorities."

Of that, for a first, no convincing was needed. "Three hundred plus interest," Seb replied. "That's my priority." Then, against better judgment, he added, "And I *will* collect." It sounded pathetic crossing his lips, but what use now was holding back?

Rich laughed, "Or you'll what?"

Footsteps chattered from the living room. Kit popped into the kitchen beside them, dressed in what looked like hospital scrubs and carrying a jar. "Dad," she said, "and Seb, listen up."

Kit was easy to ignore; Seb had made a life of it. He collected his wits: what *could* he do? There was only one equal, if not higher, power. There'd be no end to his father's shame. "I'll tell mom," he said.

Rich smiled patronizingly. "As if your mother doesn't know."

The words struck like a thunderclap.

"Dad," Kit said.

"You think this was my choice, alone?" Rich said. "You're a member of a family, Seb. Hopefully, from now on, you won't forget that."

Seb could only stand there, in checkered pajamas but otherwise naked. He'd racked his brain up and down, but rejoinders flow from hearts, not minds, and his had been demolished. *This,* at last, was rock-bottom. There was nowhere left to fall.

Kit said, "Seb."

He tuned her out. His father and mother had conspired to rob him. He could feel the tears welling, profound in their peculiar, unknown bitterness. But even now, surrender was out of the question. There was no childhood left to slink back to. He was all by himself in the world, save for the fleeting wisps of the dream. And that would have to be enough. "Then *both* of you can pay me back—"

"Richard and Sebastian Riggs!" Kit cried at the top of her lungs.

In unison, they shouted, "What?"

"Finally," Kit sighed. She meekly held aloft a jar, stuffed with twenty-dollar bills. "Seb, I have your money."

A heavy-laden silence fell, such as Seb had never known. He could feel his jaw gape to his chest, quite by its own volition. It was all so mesmerizingly strange. He'd either died and gone to purgatory, or entered *The Twilight Zone*. "You have *what?*"

Rich demanded, "Where did you get that?"

"I earned it," she said sheepishly, "candy-striping at Hawthorn Veterinary. It was the only way I could be around dogs. And I knew Seb needed it for his airplane."

Seb and Rich glared at the money: Seb in rapt astonishment; Rich, no doubt, for different reasons.

"Three hundred dollars," Kit said. "There's a little more if you need that, too."

Rich said, "My children are thieves."

Kit's eyes reddened. Seb's body tensed. He, himself, could own that label, but for Kit it was below the belt. He glared at his father. "Excuse me?"

"Or sneaks, at least," Rich said.

Same difference. Seb said, "Or self-reliant."

Rich shook his head. "You both have a lot to learn." He shoved Seb aside. "You'll thank me when you're older."

He snatched the money jar out of Kit's grasp. Kit, shrieking, re-grabbed the jar. Seb thrust his arms between the two and clasped whatever he could touch. Sobbing, Kit ripped the jar towards herself, burying her face against Seb's side. Rich thrashed away, roaring in what sounded like rage, when Seb caught a glimpse of what he'd grabbed.

It was his father's mangled hand.

"Let me go!" Rich cried in pain.

Seb said, "Let *it* go!"

Rich doubled his grip, overpowering Seb and Kit and dragging them across the room. Kit, shaking, held fast the jar. Tears congealed behind Seb's eyes. How could it have come to this?

In a twinkling, out of nowhere, he saw Ashy Larry's face; reading aloud Llewellyn's photo, freeing the ghost of a life lived in guilt. *What really matters is right beside you.* Behind Larry were Lauren and Chuck, the old soldier Osur, the birdwatcher Schultz—and, when it really mattered, even Timmy, each standing beside Seb in his time of need. Kit, now, had outshone them all. But Kit, like Seb, had had to start somewhere. And that was still worth holding on to.

"Dad," Seb said, "stop. You're better than this." He released his grip on his father's hand. "Please, you're better than this."

Rich looked at his daughter, then up at Seb, then to the money still clutched in his hands. Kit's anguished, breathless sobs filled the room. Through the ceiling-hole, the crew peered down, mortified. As he had at his shattered Dreamin' last June, Rich gazed forlornly at the jar, staring at but past it. Through his own maudlin tears inundating his eyes, Seb could have sworn he saw his father's thumbs wiggle, as if he was back in his own childhood, before life and the world had beaten him down. The world fell suddenly, eerily silent, with only the ceiling-tarp's rhythmic flapping to remind anyone that life had gone on.

Rich's grip, then body, slackened. Kit swiped away the money jar and dove behind the kitchen table.

Rich held his injured hand to his face, panting. "This is a terrible thing I've done," he said, "a terrible, terrible thing." Beneath his father's brutish eyes and knotty, sweat-soaked brow, Seb could see compassion returning. "I owe you three hundred dollars, Seb. I'll never forgive myself."

But somehow, it was no longer about money. In fact, for

all Seb cared, the fucking money could burn. "Forget it," Seb replied. "It's over. We all have blood on our hands."

Seb held out his hand. His father, nodding, took it in his. It felt dry and strong, as Osur's had felt, but also detached.

It felt like expectations.

The whirring of drills and pounding of hammers resumed from the roof. Rich turned to his daughter. "Kathryn—"

"No," Seb said, "let me."

He crouched beside his sister. "It's over now, Kit. You can come out."

She held up the money jar. "I meant it, Seb," she said between sobs. "This is for you. I'm not hearing no."

Refusal could not have been farther from mind. There was only one thing left to do: the thing that not only one wild summer but his whole life had built to. The dream was his, to have and to hold. It was all so crystal-clear.

He took his sister by the hand. "Come with me," he said. "I'll show you something cool."

xxvi.

SEPTEMBER IS a rising curtain: a time to cleanse the old for the new, a chance to get one's story straight and chart the course ahead. September is a lovers' quarrel betwixt the puerile sloth of summer and autumn's industry. September is the pulpy scent of freshly opened hand-me-down textbooks with coffee-rings and margin doodles, and the crunch of Trapper-Keeper Velcro not yet dulled by use. September is pigskins, old friends, new crushes; swimsuits stored in drawers for spring, and long, last wistful backwards looks on fated summer loves. September is mawkish melancholy, even as September's the supple springboard for all that's yet to come.

*　　　*　　　*　　　*　　　*

The backyard seemed especially lush, likely because of last weekend's rain and the incandescent sunshine that had nonstop smiled upon them since. Seb and Kit sat side-by-side, a fluffball rolling at their feet, the newest member of Family Riggs. In his adventures with Timmy, as luck would have had, Seb had met a retriever breeder and remembered a late-summer litter was due.

"You'll thank me in a week," he said. "Cornball always gives a quiz on day one."

Kit said, "So I've heard."

Mr. Cornwall's yearly reading assignment of *Henry IV, Part I* was as much the stuff of Stony Glen legend as Lloyd Llewellyn himself. "Yeah," Seb said, "but what you *haven't* been told is what he's looking for. He doesn't care if you remember names. He wants to know what you make of Prince Hal. He wants to know what growing up means to you." He'd wished someone had warned him like this exactly one year ago. But what else were big brothers for?

Kit cradled, then kissed, the bouncy puppy. "You didn't have to do this, you know."

"I know," he said. But he did. When Kit had presented her jar full of cash, there was zero doubt.

"What do you think I should name him?" she said.

A certain word seemed apropos. Life had come full-circle indeed, and all inside one summer. "How about *Dreamin'?*"

Kit scrunched her face in puzzlement. "Hmm," she said. "Yes...I think it fits him well." She scratched behind the puppy's ears. He turned and licked her hand.

A gentle breeze meandered past. Seb thought of the field where, three months before, he and his dad had watched model airplanes. That vista, like fire, was seared in his mind. His father had afterwards said something to him, but he'd be damned if he could remember what.

"Oh, well," Kit said, "happy Seb-tember."

He groaned, "You say that every year."

"Yeah," she said, "but this time I mean it."

Seb, on a lawn chair, next to his sister, was glad he was no place other than there. He patted Dreamin's furry head. Life, already plenty good, was about to get a lot more interesting. And he couldn't wait.

"You'd better," he said.

THE END

About the Author

T.G. MONAHAN is a novelist who received his B.A. from Rutgers University and his J.D. from Albany Law School. He is a former Judge Advocate officer in the U.S. Marine Corps and a veteran of the Iraq War. A native of Hawthorne, New Jersey, he now resides in Albany, New York, with his son. He is also the author of *The Vexing Heirloom*.

www.TGMonahan.com

Thank you for reading *Dreamin' in '89*. Please help us keep the spirit of the eighties alive by helping other readers find this book. Here are some suggestions for your consideration:

- Write an online customer review
  wherever books are sold

- Gift this book to family and friends

- Share a photo of the book on social media and tag
  #Dreamin89 and #TGMonahan

- Bring in T.G. Monahan as a speaker
  for your club or organization

- Suggest *Dreamin' in '89* to your local book club, and
  download the Book Club Discussion Questions from
  www.CitrinePublishing.com/bookclubs

- For more information, contact Citrine Publishing at
  (828) 585-7030 or Publisher@CitrinePublishing.com

- Connect with the author online by visiting
  www.TGMonahan.com

www.ingramcontent.com/pod-product-compliance
Lightning Source LLC
Chambersburg PA
CBHW020329260626
47156CB00004B/1439